Andrew J M

U.C.P

By

Andrew Malmquist

Copyright © 2014 Andrew J Malmquist

All rights reserved.

Prologue

There is a place located in the far north of Canada where people are sent to disappear. It is a place that only a select few know the true story of; a once booming town nestled in the wilderness far from society that had been abandoned due to the plummeting prices of the product that it was built to yield. If one was to do a search on the internet, they might discover that this place from the past still retained a population of fewer than one hundred individuals, compared to the five-thousand who once called it their home. What the results would fail to show is that these people are all employed by the Uranium City Prison or U.C.P. as some have come to call it.

U.C.P. is a privately retained facility that was founded with the support of a select few government officials in 1987. It has essentially remained non-existent in the knowledge of the world's population. For twenty-five years U.C.P. has claimed many captives; the bulk of them placed there for being threats to one influential person or another.

Chapter 1

The view out the window showed nothing more than a vast sea of snow stretching on for as far as the human eye would allow. Wes's body groaned with every bump that the bus's failed suspension cast his way. The seat he had chosen upon boarding the bus had springs protruding from the worn vinyl that had once upholstered it. Sitting as close to the window as possible was the only way to escape the unbearable jabbing that they threatened to deliver. The sad thing was that this seat had been the best out of the entire selection in the vehicle. Many aches coursed through his body from the constant abuse that continued to add up along the journey but the worst discomfort he felt was that he did not know where he was being taken.

The bus was the last in a unit of four; all of them painted white with "U.C.P." marked on the sides in faded green lettering. Although there were only five men on this bus, not including the driver, the other buses in the group were all at full capacity. Everyone had been forced onto the transport convoy at a small private airport. How all the people had ended up there Wes did not know. He had been brought to the location alone in the back of a van after being taken from his apartment in the heart of the night, then tied up and blindfolded for the entire trek. He was not sure how long it had taken to reach the airport. Time had no meaning when you were not able to keep it. Nor did it matter; there were new problems to face. Attempting an escape was an idea that hurtled through his mind but even if he was capable of coming up with a way off the bus, where would he be? The road they were cruising along had not passed any indication of civilization in what must have been hours. What they had passed had been no more than a refueling shack for the few vehicles that dared to wander this far into the Canadian north. And, there was also the fact that it was the middle of the worst winter the country had experienced in nearly a decade. Escape was not an option worth investing much thought into at this point.

The man who settled into the seat across from Wes captured his attention. He appeared almost familiar; mid-sixties, slender, balding scalp, grizzled beard, and a large horrid scar that traveled from just below his right eye to the bottom of his cheek. A sinister aura seemed to radiate off of him. Shaking off the impression of familiarity, Wes resumed his gaze out the window. In the distance structures begin to take form. Curiosity sprouted in his mind as to what exactly the place that lay ahead of them truly was. Until now, no one on the bus had dared to speak to one another but the silence was broken by the fellow with the hideous scar who whispered, *"This might be the be-all and the end-all here but here upon this bank and shoal of time, we'd jump the life to come."*

A man sitting in the next row forward spun around in his seat to face the older gentleman. In a thick Russian accent he declared, "That is very dark, my friend. I sense that you may know what is in store for us at the end of this long journey?"

The elderly man nodded. "Ah, I do. It is a place that I have been running from for nearly twenty years. Welcome to the end of the line, son, for there is no hope of ever turning back. If you look up ahead in the distance you will see a true hell on earth...Uranium City Prison...where the only way out is death." Wes shuddered at the words spoken by the old man but continued to eavesdrop on the dialogue taking place between him and the Russian.

"Sounds like you have been to this place before, Old-timer. Do you have a name? They call me Viktor."

The old man sat in silence, contemplating for a moment. Wes began to think that he would not answer Viktor's question but after what seemed like a very long lull in the conversation the old man finally gave a sigh before replying. "Over the years I have had many names but since I am headed into the final act of my life I will bring back one that I have not been called in a long, long time. You may call me Abhorson."

"Abhorson, the Executioner?"

"Something like that. Now, I suggest that you enjoy these last few minutes of peace. You may never experience the feeling again."

Viktor nodded, turning back in the direction of the front of the bus, enabling the bitter sweet sound of silence to once again creep up upon the passengers. In the tranquility of the moment Wes sought to make light of what he had heard. Uranium City Prison? A place such as that could not exist. In college he had written a paper on the prison system in Canada and no such place had ever turned up in any of the research he conducted. What was this place really…and why am I here…were questions that were bouncing around in the innermost cavities of his mind.

As the buses drew closer to their destination, Wes examined the scene. The place they were advancing on looked to be a town. Where was the so called prison? There were no walls, fences, or guard towers. People could be spotted moving around, looking as if they were going about their daily business in a normal little town. The trip was nearing an end and Abhorson's words were still resounding in his mind. Could this place be as ruthless as he made it out to be? A glimmer of faith still remained in him; the possibility that upon arrival he could explain that there had been some sort of mistake and he would be allowed to return to his home.

The busses pulled into the town, parking in a space that could be deemed a town square. There were four small booths set up along the east side of the area, one for each of the buses.

As the passengers disembarked they were directed to stand in the appropriate line. Observing his surroundings Wes could see that the men and women he had identified from a distance were actually armed guards. Distracted by the environment around him he was the final person to get into an assigned line that led to one of the booths. It did not make much of a difference though, being that there had only been the five men on his bus. The line progressed promptly. Each man received an envelope and appeared to be verified on an attendance sheet when it was their turn at the stall. The time had come; a chance for him to straighten out the predicament he was now finding himself in. Seated in the stall was a young blonde woman. Wes guessed that she was about his age; twenty-three or so. "You are the last one on my list which makes you Scott Loken, correct?"

"No! Scott is my roommate. What the hell is going on?"

"Uh oh, who are you then?"

"Wes Petersen. You didn't answer my question!"

"Well, it seems we have a problem, Mr. Petersen."

"I would say so."

"The boss will be giving a speech shortly on that stage over there," the blonde said, pointing towards a platform at the far end of the plaza. "Why don't you go watch? Afterwards, I will have someone fetch you and hopefully we can get this little complication sorted out."

"What is going on?"

"Go listen to the speech, Mr. Petersen. It may answer some of your questions."

Wes turned away, disgusted with the woman who was being of absolutely no help to him. He began pacing towards the stage, a state of overwhelming disbelief engulfing him. What kind of stuff had Scott been involved in that would warrant such a thing? As he approached the whispering crowd that had begun to assemble in front of the stage, a man in his late fifties strolled out sporting a lavish suit and a microphone in his hand. He was a tall man with a snow white beard and medium length white hair. He began to address the crowd before him, his influence blasting from two thunderous speakers, one set up on each end of the platform. His presence was that of a man who held confidence, enough that the crowd's attention was captured by the sheer sureness of the man's voice. Abruptly, the murmurs that had been taking place before the speaker's arrival diminished, leaving only the resounding sound of the bearded man's voice to be heard.

"Hello to all you fresh arrivals. My name is Mr. King. This is your new home; your last home. In your envelopes you will find directions to your new living quarters and instructions for your day tomorrow which will include being assigned to a job. This is not a regular prison; this is a society! Every one of you is here for a reason and you will all do your part. Room and board will be docked from your pay. Any extra U.C.P currency may be used to purchase extravagances such as cigarettes or candy. We do not have walls here. If anyone wishes to leave, just walk out of town and don't come back. Be warned though. You are far from civilization and, if the elements don't get you, then the wildlife will. Also, I would like to point out that if you do choose to leave then you are not welcome to return. Since today is your first day here, you may have the remaining portion of it to get acquainted with your new home. If there are any issues, please express them to one of the guards and your problems will be addressed accordingly. Welcome to Uranium City!"

When the speech was over and Mr. King withdrew from the stage, the crowd slowly began to disperse. Wes just kept standing in the same position, stunned by the reality of the kind of place that he had just ended up in. That's when he noticed the guard approaching. It was a woman outfitted in an all-black guard's uniform. A rifle was strung over her right shoulder. "Mr. Petersen?"

"Yes?"

"I need you to come with me, please. Mr. King has requested your presence."

"Good, hopefully he will get this mess straightened out and I can go home."

"Let's go," she said, ignoring Wes's comment.

The guard began to walk away. Wes had to hurry to keep pace with her. They rounded a corner. Surprisingly, an idling snowmobile sat awaiting their arrival. "So, what is your name?" Wes asked, endeavoring to generate a little small talk with his new companion.

"Amy."

"How long have you worked in this place?"

"Look, Mr. Petersen. You are a prisoner here and I am a guard. You are not supposed to talk to me. The consequence of a guard and a prisoner associating is severe. I shouldn't have even given you my name so please stop talking and hold on tight."

Before he could reply Amy gunned the throttle nearly causing him to tumble off the back of the machine. Speeding down the street at lightning speeds, it only took a few minutes before they were pulling up to the entrance of what appeared to have formerly been a school. Dismounting the snowmobile, Wes started for the entrance with Amy on his tail making sure that he did not stray from the path he was to take.

"Mr. King's office is right there." Amy uttered, indicating a door on the right side of the hall just past the confines of the foyer. Coming to a stop in front of the door, Wes reached for the knob.

"Stop!"

"Huh?" he asked, turning back to face Amy.

"You are to knock first."

"Ah." he retorted as he knocked on the frosted glass pane of the door.

"Please come in!" a loud beckoning voice called from the interior of the room. It was easily recognizable to be coming from the man he had listened too just a short period before. Obeying the command, he turned the knob, stepping into the office. Amy remained outside the room, waiting. Mr. King sat behind an enormous desk. Papers were strewn all over it in a mess that would take a team of people days to sort out. The man sitting behind the desk gestured for Wes to take a seat in one of the two wingback chairs positioned to face the bureau. "Hello Mr. Petersen. How are you?"

"I would be a hell of a lot better if you would explain to me what is going on."

"Hmm…well, what is it that you wish to know?" Mr. King asked while stroking his beard.

"For starters, why am I here?"

"There was a little bit of a mix up. You were brought here by mistake instead of your roommate, Mr. Loken."

"Why were you after him?"

"Someone wanted him to vanish."

"Who might that someone be?"

"I can't say."

"What is this place?"

"That depends who you are asking. To me, this is my place of business. To the guards, this is a place of employment. To men of money and power, this is a place where they send their problems to disappear. And, last but not least, to the prisoners, this is the end of the line. It is the last place they will ever see. I will give you one more question, Mr. Petersen, then I must return to my work."

"Since this is a mistake, when can I leave?"

"That seems to me a waste of a question. Were you not listening to my welcome speech? You are free to leave anytime. There are no walls or fences here to stop you. If you wish to go, then feel free to leave. If not, since this is somewhat the fault of some incompetent employees of mine, then you may take Mr. Loken's place here. Now, have a good day, Mr. Petersen." A large grin appeared on Mr. King's face as he finished speaking.

"You can't do this...!" Wes started to shout from his chair.

"Miss Kale!" hollered Mr. King, interrupting him mid-sentence. In an instant Amy was in the room standing in between the chairs, ready to obey any command that might be bequeathed to her. "Ah, Miss Kale, swift as always, I see. Could you please escort Mr. Petersen to his residence? He will be replacing Scott Loken, so please make sure that everything regarding this matter is dealt with appropriately. We don't want any more problems that have to be addressed when it comes to Mr. Petersen's identity."

"Of course, leave it to me, Sir." She shoved Wes towards the door, following orders like an obedient hound. Glancing back towards the man behind the desk one final time, Wes was able to catch Mr. King's final quip. "Good day to you, Mr. Petersen."

With a final shove, Amy succeeded in moving Wes beyond the confines of the office. She stepped out behind him closing the door with delicacy so that it did not even create the slightest sound. He was about to say something to her, then thought better of it as he did not wish to cause her any trouble. It was not her fault he was caught up in this predicament. She was only doing her job.

As Amy accompanied him to what was to be his new home, he got the feeling that she had heard the exchange of conversation between him and Mr. King. He waited for her to mention something in regards to his predicament but she did not. She remained quiet as they rode back through the center of town. Everyone had cleared out of the vicinity by this point in time, obviously headed to check out their own assigned living arrangements. Once reaching the other side of the town they came to what looked like a small apartment building. She brought the sled to a stop just outside the front doors. Getting off,

Wes turned to her for further instruction. "You are in apartment 4A, Mr. Petersen," she informed him while handing over an envelope and a key.

"Um, thanks, I guess."

"Good luck," she whispered under her breath as she slowly pulled away.

Catching a glimpse of pity in her eyes as she left, Wes turned to face the building he was now supposed to live in. It was made of red brick and appeared as if maintenance was far from a priority. Dead shrubs and debris were piled along the exterior of the apartment buildings walls. Taking a deep breath, he strode through the front doors. The décor in the lobby appeared to all be from the seventies, right from the wall paper to the few furnishings that had been placed about to make the place feel more inviting. It made Wes feel as if he had stepped back a couple of generations in time. There was a staircase located on the right side of the room. Before entering he had counted the number of floors that the building had. There were four, which put his new home on the top level of the structure. Taking his time he ascended the stairs, unsure of what to expect when he reached his apartment at the top.

At the peak of the staircase he spotted his door which was located directly across from where the stairs came out on the fourth floor. The door was covered in black peeling paint with brass lettering screwed into the old wood indicating that it was indeed apartment 4A. As he approached the door, he stuck the key Amy had given him into the lock and, turning it, the latch released. The door whined on its hinges as it was pushed open. Walking into the apartment, he soaked in his surroundings. Just as the lobby had been, it seemed that everything in the room had been pulled straight out of the past. A dim lamp endeavored to illuminate the room, casting eerie shadows along the walls of faded color. Just then he noticed the man sitting in the chair facing the window; his feet perched on the sill, a pipe suspended from his mouth. He was almost hidden by the shadows the weak lighting failed to chase away. "Umm, hello?" he said in a questioning voice to the man he had just intruded on.

"Can I help you?" asked the man, a puff of smoke rising up from his mouth as he spoke.

"I was told that this is where I am supposed to live."

"You can have that room." The man pointed at one of three doors that exited off the living room area. While he talked, another waft of smoke escaped from between his parted lips.

"My name is Wes."

"That's nice."

"It looks like we are going to be roommates. Are you not going to tell me your name?"

"Jack, not that it matters though. You will be dead soon enough. My last flat-mate lasted just over a week before he went and got himself killed."

"How was he killed?"

"He spoke to the wrong person. For that he was hanged."

"That can't be right. It's against the law."

"You better realize real fast if you want to survive here; laws have no effect in this place. This prison does not really exist."

"Hmm…why are you here?"

"I have to go. My shift starts shortly. Make yourself at home," explained Jack as he stood up and advanced towards the front door in a successful attempt to avoid answering any more questions.

"But…" It was too late. Jack had slammed the door cutting Wes off from any more conversation and Wes was left standing in the center of the room, confused by the sheer lack of information that he had been able to get out of the people he had come across since arriving in the prison. Brushing it off, he decided to check out his newly acquired room.

Just like the front door had, the bedroom door moaned on its hinges as it swung open. The room was small. Just as everything else had been so far, it looked as if it too had been furnished many years ago. There was a single bed covered with an ancient yellowing quilt tucked away in a corner. Next to the bed was a rickety old night stand with an alarm clock resting on its surface. The opposite side of the room accommodated a chest of drawers. It was missing all the handles except for one on the bottom drawer. There were no windows in this room and the only light came from a single bulb suspended from the ceiling. Sitting down on the bed Wes unsealed the envelope that Amy had given him. It contained general information such as eating times, a map of the prison, and a location of where to meet for starting work the next day. According to the instructions he was to be outside the dining hall at seven in the morning to board a bus that would take him to his assigned mine. Nowhere in the envelope's contents was it mentioned what exactly he would be doing at the mine, but he didn't imagine that it was going to be pleasant. Then he remembered what he had heard earlier during the speech; that positions would be assigned the following day.

Glancing at the time displayed on the alarm clock Wes realized that it was too late for dinner. As he had read on one of the documents in his packet the hall closed at nine in the evening. It was now nine-thirty. Not a big deal though as he did not possess much of an appetite with all that was transpiring around him. So in lieu of going for dinner he undressed and proceeded to crawl under the somewhat musty smelling covers on his bed. Closing his eyes, he braced for what the next day might have in store for him while he waited for sleep to take him away.

Chapter 2

The alarm clock went off; screaming in Wes's ear. Without opening his eyes he reached over, slamming his hand down on the snooze button. As he lay in peace he replayed a dream that had come during the night, trying to decipher its meaning. In it, he had dreamed of being abducted in the in the middle of the night, taken from his home and escorted to a faraway prison. The dream had been extremely vivid, as if it were not a dream at all.

Once again the clock came to life, threatening the best interest of his ear drums with its insistent sounds. Just as before, he reached over hitting the snooze button and resuming the alarm's slumber. Calmness again filled the room. Something didn't seem to add up though. There was a lack of noise. Where was the usual sound of the morning traffic passing by on the street below his apartment? Opening his eyes, he realized that he had forgotten to turn off the light before he had gone to bed the night before. Slowly they adjusted to the brightness and everything came reeling back. There had been no dream about being sent away to some horrible prison. What had seemed to be an unrealistic night terror was in fact a reality.

Shutting the alarm off properly to prevent it from disturbing the peace a third time, Wes swung his legs off the side of the bed. The room was very chilly and when he thought of getting dressed he realized that the only clothes he had were the ones he had worn to bed the night he was taken. With a little disgust, he dressed in the soiled clothing. Looking at the clock, it read 6:20 giving him a little time before he was due to be picked up for his first day of work at the mines. After using the washroom in the apartment he headed for the dining hall.

The morning air was crisp but the sky was clear. It allowed him to gaze at the northern lights as they danced across the still darkened sky. According to the map from the envelope the hall was located near the center of town, making the walk just a short distance. It was housed in what was an old ice rink, possibly meant for curling. The area was abuzz with people.

Entering through the front door Wes stepped into a room with a hundred tables or so spread throughout. Just about all of the tables had people seated around them. A line on the left side of the room took people past a window where they were served a plate of breakfast. His stomach rumbled as he got in line. It had been a very long time since it had received the comforting nourishment of food and it was now making a verbal statement in protest to any more starvation. The line moved fast. When he got to the window he was handed a plate of food along with a set of utensils. On the plate rested two fried eggs, three small slices of bacon, and a blackened piece of toast.

Looking around the room he spotted one of the few empty tables. He made his move, weaselling his way through the slew of people to claim a seat at it. While sitting there semi enjoying the filling feeling that the tasteless food provided him, someone set a folded napkin down on the table beside him as they walked past. Glancing up, he was able to catch a glimpse of the man before he vanished into the mass of people that filled the room. It was Viktor, the Russian man from the bus. Picking up the napkin, he unfolded it to reveal a roughly scribbled note. It read; "Town center,

10pm. Come alone." Discreetly, he tucked the note into his pocket.

Nobody joined Wes at his table during his meal. Once he had finished eating he carried his dirty dishes over to a cart by the entrance as he had noticed others had done when they had finished with their meals. Figuring it must be getting close to seven o'clock, he joined a group of other prisoners who were gathered in front of the hall waiting for their transport to arrive. Conversation was something that evaded the group however it was only a matter of a few minutes before two buses pulled up. They were full of passengers coming back from the night shift. Wes spotted Jack amongst the crowd that disembarked. Everyone who was just arriving headed into the building to conquer their appetites after a long nights work. Once the busses were empty the men working the day shift began to climb aboard, Wes included. The busses were identical to the ones that had brought the new prisoners the day before. Perhaps they were even the same ones. Once packed full, the engines roared to life as the driver pressed his foot down on the gas pedal causing the vehicle to lurch forward.

It was still dark out so there was nothing that one could see through the windows as the bus putted along the dirt road towards the mine site. The ride was only a short way, taking about fifteen minutes to arrive from the time it departed.

The equipment compound at the site was lit up like a Christmas tree as the bus rolled through its gates. There were lights set up everywhere so that not a single shadow dared to exist in the confines of the yard's fences. Machinery was scattered about; some of it looked operable and the rest appeared to be barely usable for parts. In the middle of the yard the busses came to a halt. The driver reached over and pulled a lever, opening the door so that his captives could be released into the compound. While everyone else was off and running to their posts, Wes just stood outside his bus, unsure of where he was supposed to go or who to report to. He must have been the only one of the new arrivals to be assigned to this crew because he imagined that if he wasn't he would not be standing all by himself.

"Mr. Petersen!" a man called as he came walking over from a small rundown building that was presumably used as an office.

"Yes?" replied Wes, turning his attention to the short, chubby man approaching him from across the yard site.

"My name is Arnold Dunn and I am the site foreman."

"Um, ok."

"Come with me over to the safety shack and we can get you set up for work."

Doing as directed he followed the short man as he waddled back towards the shack he had come from. It was no issue keeping up since the man's stubby legs prevented him from moving at a pace any faster than what the average person would consider slow. Tossing the door to the building open, Arnold entered. Wes followed him inside, shutting the door behind him as he entered.

"Take a seat, Mr. Petersen." Mr. Dunn instructed, while pointing at a large table with a dozen folding chairs set up around it.

Doing as he was told, Wes sat. He looked around the room taking in a visual of it while he waited for his host to sit down on the opposite side of the table. The shack was old and dirty. Tools strewn about, dirty coveralls piled in a corner and an overflowing garbage can were all sights that could be observed in the haggard heap of a building.

"So, Mr. Petersen, what is it that you did before coming here to the prison?

"I did some freelance writing for a magazine."

"Hmm…there's nothing like that around here. Do you have any mechanical experience?"

"No sir, never even owned a vehicle."

"Hmm…well, we had an old feller who was our tag man but he had a heart attack a few days back and sadly he didn't make it. It's an easy job. I would put you in the mine but you're a scrawny one and you would get yourself killed in no time if I went and did something like that. Do you know what a tag man does?"

"I don't."

"Well, you see, a tag man sits in a little booth at the entrance to the mine. Every man who comes to you receives a tag and you write down his name and tag number. At the end of the day he returns the tag and you check him off the list. That way we know if anyone else is still in the mine. Do you think you can handle that?"

"Sounds easy."

"Is that a yes?"

"Yes."

"Good, now get over there and start before the men begin heading into the mine. They are all over getting their gear together at the moment so if you hurry you should be able to beat them over there before they show up to get their tags."

"Ok, is everything I need in the booth?"

"Yeah, get over there now!"

Without another word, Wes stood up and went outside. Looking across the yard he could see the little shack that Arnold Dunn had stationed him at. Sprinting towards it he noticed the truly repulsive nature of its looks. Every step closer showed even more detail of the state of decay the shack was in. The door was busted off on its lower hinge causing it to hang in a lackadaisical fashion. On arrival he pulled it open carefully so that he would not damage it any further than it already was and stepped inside. The room was small, maybe six feet by eight feet. On the one wall was an opening where the miners could line up to receive and return their tags, somewhat like the kitchen in the dining hall. Everything in this place was set up to run efficiently. The opposite wall held a rack where all the tags were hung in numerical order waiting for use. The only furnishings were a tall wooden table by the window opening and a rickety old handmade wood stool to sit on. Atop the table sat some notebooks and pens. Wes also noted a big green coat hooked on a nail by the door. It looked well used but he was cold and definitely planned to use it. Grabbing the coat he pulled it around himself. It was frigid from being exposed to the elements but it would not take long for his body heat to warm up its fabric. Then, as if on cue, the first of the miners arrived at the window. He asked the miner for his name, jotting it down in one of the notebooks as the man gave it. He then handed the miner a tag, number forty-seven, scribbling the number beside the name in the notebook as the miner left for the mine. The task was repeated over and over again with every individual who had to enter the mine. Then he sat on his stool and waited. There was no one else to hand a tag out to and there would be no returns until the end of the day. The job was turning out to be quite boring.

All day he sat by himself, shivering in the little depilated shack and thinking about how he was going to get himself out of this mess and return back to civilization. The only thing he did in the afternoon was hand out a tag to the guy who brought lunch for him and the miners. When he came out of the mine Wes returned the man's tag to the wall, making a check mark on his list to show the man had returned. The lunch was the same for everyone on shift. It consisted of a bologna sandwich, a bottle of water, and a granola bar.

Slowly picking away at his food, he waited for the men to surface at the end of the work day. Finally, after hours of sitting on his stool doing nothing but playing games in his mind, a group of the miners came strolling out of the depths. They were very dirty and all wearing the same look of exhaustion. One by one their tags were returned to the wall, a check going beside each name until every man was accounted for. Once done, Wes left the shack and headed over to climb aboard his ride back to town. He was one of the last to board the bus due to the nature of the position he was assigned. Just as it had been on the way out to the mine, the trip back was engulfed in the darkness that was brought on by the dwindling hours of the day. All that he wanted to do was go back to his quarters, take a hot shower, and crawl into bed. Then he remembered the note from Viktor in his pocket and he realized that sleep would have to wait.

When the bus arrived back at the dining hall, most of the passengers headed in to claim their dinner immediately. Wes decided that he would head straight back over to the apartment and take a shower before returning for something to sooth his starving belly. Walking briskly had him at the flat in no time. He jogged up the stairs and went into the apartment. As he entered, he noticed a young Asian man talking to Jack.

"Sounds good, Jack."

"See you tomorrow," Jack said as the Asian man hurried past Wes and out the door without even acknowledging his presence.

"Um, hey, Jack. I want a shower. Is there a towel I could use?"

"There is a box in the closet over there. It has a towel and some clothes that may fit you. It belonged to my previous roommate but you are more than welcome to it." Jack said, pointing at the closet in the entryway of the apartment.

"Thanks…who was that guy that was just here?"

"Just a friend."

"Ok," Wes answered, thinking it looked a little suspicious. He walked over to the closet, taking out the box of stuff that belonged to someone who would never again need its contents. He took it straight into the washroom with him, setting it on the counter. Opening it he found a towel, a couple of t-shirts, a sweater, wool socks, two pairs of jeans and a belt. Although the jeans were a size or two too big around the waist, the belt would solve that issue.

"Be warned! We don't have the pleasure of having hot water here!" called Jack from the other room.

"Of course not," he muttered to himself as he prepared for his shower. Climbing in, he shivered as the ice cold water came in contact with his skin. The sensation was almost painful but Wes felt dirty and was compelled to rinse away the grime that had accumulated since his last shower. Keeping it short, he only remained under the water long enough to give himself a quick but thorough rinse. Then he was out and drying off, shaking from the chill the water had left him with. Maybe the place truly was hell; it just starts with small things, poor tasting food and no hot water. He wondered what he would come across next. The adopted clothes didn't fit well but it was better than wearing what he had previously had on as it was beginning to smell quite rank from lack of washing. After dressing, the chill from the cold began to dissipate. With a feeling of being semi clean Wes headed off to procure himself some dinner. He had been unable to wash properly due to the lack of soap.

On the walk towards the hall Wes looked up into the sky. The night was cloudless, allowing the stars to shine bright. It was unlike any sight he had ever experienced before. Growing up in the city, the picturesque beauty the night offered was hidden by the street lights and the ever increasing smog. Had he not stepped on a patch of ice and nearly slipped and fallen, his gaze could have been entangled within the mesmerizing power of the stars for eternity.

The hall seemed less busy than it had been earlier in the evening when the crew had first arrived back from the mine. Entering, Wes estimated that there were approximately twenty people sitting around tables dining. There wasn't even a line at the counter to slow him down on receiving his plate of food this time. On the plate he received a baked potato, creamed corn and a pork chop. The food smelled great but just looking at it he could tell that it was a very generic concoction which was created to serve a large group their basic requirements and not as something to be enjoyed. Once again he took a seat at a table by himself, eating his very mediocre food in silence. Even at the tables that housed multiple people, conversation was kept at a minimum.

A clock on the wall informed Wes that it was just past quarter after eight. He still had a fair amount of time before he was due to have his meeting at ten. Wondering if there were any evening activities that he could partake in, he decided to ask one of the other dinner patrons after dropping his dirty dishes over at the cart he had seen and used that very morning. A man was seated by himself near the exit. He was wearing a black toque with a red and black plaid jacket and appeared to be a perfect target to attempt to create a little conversation.

"Excuse me, sir?" Wes inquired as he approached.

"What do you want?"

"Is there anything to do here, something to possibly kill some time?"

"Yes."

"Well, what are my options?"

"If you have to ask, then you have none!"

"What do you mean?"

"Once people get to know you a little and learn that you are not some sort of spy for the King, then there is the chance that you may get an invite to an activity or two."

"What kind of activity?"

"Why, tea parties of course, you idiot!"

"Whoa, I was just asking."

"Well, don't. Asking too many questions is a good way to get yourself killed...so, bugger off!"

Not wanting to cause any further disruption, Wes left without another word and made his way out onto the street. Since there was still time to kill, he thought he would explore the town, or prison, depending on how one thought of it. All the buildings were aging. The ones that looked to be in use were in fair condition but there were many that looked unused that were plagued with broken windows, peeling paint, and rotten timber. Some of the better kept buildings sported signs in the windows. Wes discovered a barber shop, general store, and a library in the small area he covered during his walk. After venturing around, it was nearly time for the supposed meeting so he proceeded to return to the town center area by the hall. It only took a few minutes as he had not strayed too far on his little exploring mission. No one was around so he made use of a bench that sat outside what looked like it might have been a little café sometime in the past. Getting comfortable on the bench, he again turned his gaze to the stars cast out across the night sky. They were just so majestic that he could not resist the temptation to do so. His trance was interrupted when someone sat down beside him, their face hidden behind a ski mask. He was unsure if it was to keep their identity unknown or to protect their skin from the biting cold. Possibly it was for both? The only feature he was able to make out were the person's icy blue eyes. They sat for a moment, eyes locked on one another. Neither of them spoke. After a few minutes passed the masked person handed Wes a toque and a pair of gloves. Taking them, he made quick use by immediately putting them on to help fend off the attacking winter air. He was about to thank the individual for the gifts but the masked person raised a finger to where their mouth was hidden behind the mask in an action that instructed him to remain quiet. The person then stood up before rushing off down an alley behind one of the many derelict structures.

"Wait!" called Wes, but his voice echoed off into the nothingness that was the night.

It was only a moment later when the man with the scar, known as Abhorson, stepped out from the shadows. He used an old wooden cane as he made his way over to take a seat where the person in the mask had been sitting just moments before. "Who were you calling out to, son?"

"I don't know who it was, but never mind that. What are you doing here?"

"We have a scheduled meeting, do we not?"

"The meeting is with you?"

"Well, do you see anyone else meeting you here at this time?"

"Well…um, no, what is it that you want?"

"I want to know if you can be trusted."

"Trusted with what?"

"You see, your friend Scott was supposed to be here for a reason. Yet, here you are in his place. I had hired him to come here and help me destroy what this so-called Mr. King has built. I need to know if you can do Scott's job."

"What was his role in this arrangement?"

"Why, he was to get on the King's good side and work his way into his circle of trust, a spy of sorts."

"What would I get out of this deal?"

"You would get your freedom and a way home. Also, since you are a writer, you would get first crack at the story of a lifetime. Imagine the career boost a story like this would give you."

"You guarantee me a way home?"

"I do."

"Then I guess I don't have a choice!"

"Excellent." The old man stood up, reaching out to shake his hand. He accepted the gesture, offering his hand back in return. A deal was struck. Wes released his grip, but Abhorson held on for a moment longer, staring down at the new gloves Wes was sporting. "I will be in touch Mr. Petersen." The old man said as he finally released his hold, then turned away to walk off into the shadows, disappearing just as suddenly as he appeared when he had first arrived.

Staying on the bench awhile longer, Wes's mind made an attempt to grasp what had just transpired around him. Who was the masked individual? What exactly was Abhorson's plan? Why was he doing it? Things were complicated, and he did not have the energy to invest into the many unanswered questions that were floating around in his head. The morning would be fast approaching, which meant that he had his second shift at the mine. With that in mind, he stood up to begin his stroll back too what he now was forced to consider his temporary home.

Chapter 3

That night sleep evaded Wes. All the unanswered questions resounded throughout his mind but it was more to do with the person in the mask than about Abhorson. At least he knew who Abhorson was. The person in the mask was completely unknown to him, thus making the fact that he was being helped by this individual a major question to which he wanted an answer.

When morning finally arrived accompanied by the ringing of the alarm clock, sleep had only just begun. Wes's eyes were droopy as he climbed out of his bed and proceeded to get redressed in the clothes that he had put on fresh the night before. After the task was complete; he went outdoors, his movements resembling that of a zombie fresh from crawling out of a grave. The morning brought a new layer of fresh snow and when Wes stepped out onto the front step of the building he slipped, falling face first into the white powder. No longer was he plagued by tiredness, the cold against his skin woke him faster than any coffee ever could. It was as rude a wakening as there ever was.

Getting up and dusting himself off while grumbling, Wes continued on his way to fetch himself some breakfast before he had to leave for the mine. Just as the previous morning, the dining hall was packed full of people preparing to leave for their own shifts at the mines. After retrieving his meal, he spotted Viktor across the room sitting alone at a table. Joining him, Viktor glared at Wes as he took a seat, obviously not wanting to be bothered. But the Russian's glare did not faze him. He knew that Viktor might have some of the answers he was looking for.

"Don't sit here. If you want to talk, I will meet you later. People will get suspicious if they see us together" commanded Viktor.

Casually, Wes did as he was told and stood up to take his breakfast and eat elsewhere. No one took notice of him and the fact that he had only just taken a seat and was already getting up from it. In fact, nobody was looking in their direction at all. He got the feeling that Viktor was just making him move in order to get rid of him so that he would not have to face any questions that may be directed towards him.

"Actually, no! I want some answers from you now." retorted Wes as he sat back down allowing his eyes to meet Viktor's gaze.

A look of surprise crossed the Russians face. "Ah, you have some back bone in ya."

"Who is Abhorson?"

"He is but a mere man."

"Shut up, you know what I mean. Now tell me what I want to know!" Wes replied while clenching his fists under the table in an attempt to control his frustration.

"Stop contradicting yourself, my friend. Do you wish for me to shut up or to tell you?" Victor said, a large grin appearing on his face as he spoke.

"Tell me."

"I cannot do that. If you have questions, you must ask Abhorson. And no, I do not know where he is. When he wants something he comes and finds me, as he will do with you."

Even more frustrated, Wes dug his fork into one of the sausages on his plate, juice squirting out and leaving a grease stain on the table cloth where it landed. Time was limited on this morning as he had a bus to catch. It could take hours or even days to get anything out of Viktor. The man was very tight lipped and it would be best to save his energy for the day ahead.

The rest of the meal was finished in silence. Viktor was the first to be done and he hurried across the room only to disappear out the door. Wes sat for a few more minutes so he wouldn't draw any attention to himself by leaving right after Viktor.

Heading outside to catch the bus he noticed that the snowfall had picked up. Large flakes were now coming down at an alarming rate. The wind was also starting to increase in velocity only to make the weather situation worse. Feeling grateful for the generosity of the unknown person from the night before would be an understatement as to what he felt towards the individual as he pulled on his gloves to shield his hands from the harsh winter weather.

Although the bus was bitterly cold on the inside it was a relief to be out of the raging wind that was still increasing in strength. With the ever growing power of the storm, visibility slowly crawled from slight to none resulting in a slow, daunting trip out to the site. What had taken a mere fifteen minutes the day before was increased to a time of just under an hour. He was now almost jealous of the other prisoners as they filed off the bus. At least they were headed into the mine and would be sheltered from the storms wake.

The morning routine went smoothly. All the men came and received their tags before heading into the shafts for the day. Well, all accept one. Wes cross-referenced with his list from the day before and found the missing miner's name was Billy. He remembered him; he had looked to be the youngest of the group, probably only sixteen or seventeen years old. There was the chance that he might be sick and he wondered if prisoners were allowed to take sick days. It was a question he figured he should look into in case he ever found himself in a situation when he may need one; however he did have a suspicion that not showing up to work even if you were sick would have dire consequences.

The day was proving to be as uneventful as the previous had been only on this day the snow continued to pile up, its harshness complimented by the consistent roaring of the wind. All that could be done was to huddle in the little ramshackle shack and try to keep from freezing. In the midst of the constant shivering, the thoughts of the boy who failed to show up for work that morning slipped away.

Late in the afternoon Dunn had waded through the snow out to the tag shack to inform Wes that there was going to be an assembly in the square at nine that evening. Dunn then proceeded to instruct him to inform all the other prisoners as they came out of the mine so when everyone came to return their tags at the end of the day the message was relayed onto them.

By the time the work day came to an end the storm was just reaching its peak. A pickup truck with a plow mounted to the front was sent to accompany the busses back to town. On route back to the town whispers moved between the passengers of the bus. Wes was left out of the conversations that passed from ear to ear. It was no surprise to him though;

he knew he was the outsider among the group. Who knew how long they had been working together building friendships and alliances while they all waited for the end to come?

At the hall, a notice was posted on the front door explaining that the night shift was cancelled in lieu of the assembly. Wes entered and found himself a seat after retrieving his food. It was not long after sitting down that Jack came and joined him at his table. For the first few minutes they ate in silence. Then Jack spoke up, "Tonight, I have a feeling you will get to see a little bit of the true nature of this place."

"Why do you say that?"

"When the King calls an assembly it usually does not result in something good, especially when he cancels one of the shifts to give it."

"What do you think it is about?"

"I don't know, but I do know that everyone is required to attend. That should put about five hundred of us all gathered in the square for it, plus the guards."

"Five Hundred?" Wes asked in astonishment.

"Yes, there is more than one mine operating. The shifts are arranged so that everyone is not doing the same things at the same time. The design they have set up is flawless however it really dims the picture for everyone here as to how big this operation really is."

"Wow."

"Just make sure that you show up for whatever performance the King has in mind. If you are caught not attending who knows what kind of punishment might befall you?

"Thanks for the tip."

"No problem" Jack replied just before he gobbled up the last few morsels of his meal. Just as abruptly as he had come, he was gone. No goodbyes were uttered. Jack had vanished in the sea of the increasing dinner crowd and Wes had a table all to himself once again.

After his meal, he decided to go check out the library he had stumbled upon the night before while he was killing time before meeting with Abhorson. It would be good if he could scavenge a book or two to read in the evenings rather than being left to mull over his own depressing thoughts. Lights could be seen inside as he approached the building that housed the library. When he reached the front door he found it unlocked. Just inside sat a table with a little sign that read, "Help yourself but only borrow one book at a time please." From the front of the room, rows of books could be seen but none of them looked to be shelved in any particular order. All of the volumes were just shoved on the shelves in any old fashion and some were even backwards or upside down. Overlooking the disorganization of it all, the selection did appear to be quite extensive.

Moving to the back of the aisles he found a table with some chairs around it. Selecting a book on the origins of vampires he sat down to read. At the very least it would kill some time before he had to join the others for the required gathering that the King called. Even though he found it disturbing he realized that he too now thought of him as "The King" instead of Mr. King.

A few pages into the book the lights mysteriously went out. Looking up in a slight bout of panic he could see nothing as the room was pitch black. Sitting still, he waited for the power to resume and just as suddenly as they had shut off, the lights flickered back on. His eyes immediately focused on a little black book that had materialized before him on the table. There was no way he could be mistaken, he was sure it had not been there before. Staring at it, curious as to where it came from, he heard the front door open and close and the little bell that chimed as it did so.

Wes jumped up from his seat knocking the chair over as he bolted for the entrance trying to catch a glimpse of the culprit responsible for turning off the power and placing the book in front of him. Stepping out through the door onto the street he was faced with the blinding snow. Through the haze of the winter wrath, he caught a glimpse of the person in the mask from the night before standing at the entrance of an alleyway a little ways down the block and staring right back at him. A friendly wave was given by the one in the mask before dashing behind a building and out of sight. Returning to the Library, Wes was going mad with curiosity as to who this masked person was. Maybe the book that was left for him would hold a clue. Manoeuvring his way through the aisles back to the table he imagined what information would come to light after examining its contents.

There it was resting on the table just as it had when it appeared during the moments of darkness. Cautiously he reached for it as if it was going to jump up and bite him. The book was cold to the touch, giving the impression that it was brought in from outside rather than originating from one of the shelves in the library. Opening the book to the first page, he found the contents had been hand written. Without reading, he flipped through the pages to see what else was contained inside. Only the first two pages held ink, the first page was simple instructions. The book was to be put into the bottom drawer of a desk located on the east side of the building after he was done reading the note thus allowing for further contact to be made through the same method if necessary. On the second page he read the scrawl out loud to himself.

> *Wes,*
>
> *I have been watching you. I know who you are and that you are not supposed to be here. Currently I am working on a way to get you home.*
>
> *Although you may have thought what you did today may bring you closer to your*

> *goal of escaping all you did was cause harm. Mr. King is not easily persuaded into trust so, if this is a plan of some sort to gain his good graces, it will be a long and dark road. Be careful for, as a result of your actions you made many enemies today.*
>
> *Sincerely,*
>
> *Anonymous*

Who was this "Anonymous" person? And what was the meaning of the reference to the day's actions? All he did was go to the mine and sit around all day before returning back to town. How could he have done something wrong during that time? The book had answered none of his questions. It only created more questions, none of which he knew the answer to.

Glancing up towards the clock that hung on the wall, Wes realized that time had flown by while he had sat contemplating the note and its meaning. It was now time to attend the gathering at the town center. Making sure to put the book in the drawer as directed, he left the library to make the short journey through the storm. Upon arriving, a large crowd had already formed. He stood at the back of it, trying to blend in amongst the mass of prisoners. Everyone was looking up at the platform that had been the stage for the King's speech only two days before. A change had been made, one that drew the attention of every human standing in the cold bleary square, a hangman's gallows now stood on the platform. A noose dangled from the peak of the structure. The very sight was disturbing. "Could this be some kind of joke?" he wondered out loud.

"I have seen a lot of crazy things in my time but this is an unheard of form of cruelty in this day and age" stated a man standing beside Wes to no one in particular.

A chill ran down Wes's spine simultaneously as the King walked out onto the stage. He was followed by two guards in standard black U.C.P uniforms who were escorting a man with a hood pulled over his head.

"Hello citizens of Uranium City! Yesterday morning one of my snowmobiles was stolen. I know…I know…who would do such a thing after all I have done for you people? But there is good news. Last night one of my guards came to me and told me the name of the thief. It seems that the man had been bragging to some others about how he was going to escape with a snowmobile that he managed to acquire. Because I was informed of this injustice I was able to have my men detain this horrible excuse of a human being." exclaimed the King, as he pointed at the man with the cover over his head. Then, with a quick motion of the King's hand the guards removed the hood showing the identity of him to the crowd.

Immediately Wes recognized the person standing on the stage as the kid who failed to show up for work at the mine earlier that day. Whispers began to flow through the crowd like a wave but no one's eyes dared to move away from the drama unfolding on the stage before them.

"Be quiet!" commanded the King, causing the whisper of voices in the crowd to fade out. "This is Billy. Had we not had this miracle of a storm, I am afraid Billy may have run off with that machine that he stole. As punishment for his actions, he is to be put to death!" The King paused for the effect of his statement to register in the minds of his audience. "In order to prevent this from happening again, I want you all to witness the punishment for this horrendous act!" After another brief pause the King placed an order with the guards, "Hang him!"

Everyone watched in horror as the two guards shoved Billy towards the noose. He did not resist. Placing it around his neck they then made their way over to a rope and began pulling it, hoisting the poor boy up into the air. Billy's body convulsed as the last of his life drained out of him. Without letting the limp body down, the guards tied off the rope leaving the lifeless body suspended in the air for all to see. The guards then turned and walked off the stage, not even offering a glance back towards the boy they had just killed.

The King turned his attention away from the corpse and returned his focus to his subjects smiling as he began to speak again. "I think he makes a nice decoration, don't you?" he asked. Not a single soul offered a response to the question. "Well, since I hear no objections I will let him hang there for a few days as a reminder. Don't worry; the cold will keep him fresh. I wouldn't want to stink up this beautiful town." Again the King grinned. "I have one last matter of business. I want to thank the man who was responsible for helping me capture this criminal by leaving a note with one of my guards. So, thank you, Wes Petersen! You are an asset to this society. As a reward you may have twenty-four hours in the executive suite and you will receive the day off from the mine tomorrow. Please head over to the dinner hall where I will have someone meet you to escort you to your suite for the night.

Wes's jaw dropped. He had no idea what the King was talking about. He had done no such thing. Looking around he watched as everyone's gaze turned on him. It started with the few people he had met so far and everyone else followed their line of sight until they too were focused on him. Their eyes were all full of hate at the betrayal, all except one individual. Wes spotted him standing about fifty feet away through the crowd, the scar on his face sticking out like a sore thumb in the poorly lit area. Abhorson was gleaming with joy. It must have been him who sent the note, he thought. This must have been part of the plan to get in good with the King. Anger was building inside and he wanted to strangle the old man who had just single handily turned every other prisoner in the town against him, but there was nothing that could be done at the moment. He had a mass of people around him who probably wanted him dead and he knew the only thing he could do to keep himself safe for the time being was to go meet with whichever guard the King had assigned for him to rendezvous with at the hall.

It may have been only a hundred feet or so across the square to the meeting point, but it felt like ten miles. People were starting to disperse but not one soul took their eyes from the man they believed to be partially responsible for the evening's events. Just as expected someone was waiting outside the hall. It was Amy, the guard he had dealt with on his first day in the prison. Her face showed no emotion even though what had happened would have bothered the most hardened souls of the criminals lost to Uranium City prison. He wondered if, deep down, what the King had just done bothered her, and the other guards for that matter. They couldn't all be crazy enough to be in line with the King's views, could they?

"Don't talk and come with me" instructed Amy as she led him to the awaiting snowmobile.

"But..."

"I said don't talk, Mr. Petersen."

Doing as he was told he remained quiet for the entire trip to the so called executive suite. It was a small house located just outside of the town. Amy led him in through the front door after they arrived. "Here is your reward for your troubles. You will find a king size bed in the bedroom and a Jacuzzi tub in the bathroom. Also, you are invited to dine with Mr. King tonight. As for breakfast and lunch tomorrow, it will be delivered to you here. For entertainment there is a TV and DVD player along with a small selection of movies, all located in the bedroom."

"I already had dinner" Wes tried to explain.

"I suggest you eat again, Mr. Petersen, as Mr. King does not like his invitations to be declined."

"I understand."

"Good, I will be back in an hour to take you to Mr. King's home."

"It is a little late for eating, don't you think?"

"Don't ask questions. The answers around here are never what you want them to be." Amy finished speaking then stepped out the door leaving him by himself inside the small house.

Without wasting another second he headed into the bathroom to check out the tub. It was equipped with seven jets. The only question was did he have access to hot water? Turning the tap on and placing his hand underneath the running water he was pleased to feel the heat of the liquid running between his fingers. Plugging the drain, he allowed the tub to fill with the steaming hot liquid as it flowed from the tap. Under the sink he found soap and shampoo. It would be refreshing to feel truly clean again.

The bath was amazing and its warmth around his body enveloped his senses. Even the aches that had accumulated over the past days where tended to by the massaging pressure of the tub's jets. Time was of no concern while he soaked, almost forgetting about his problems as he did so, until Amy burst through the bathroom door bringing reality crashing back down.

"Whoa, what the hell?" a surprised Wes asked, stunned by the intrusion.

"We are going to be late. Oh, and Mr. King wishes that you wear this" explained Amy as she set a stack of clothes down on the counter. She had changed out of her guards uniform and was now very formally dressed. Once she was sure he was going to get out of the tub and get dressed she left the room so he would have some privacy as he did so.

The King had sent over a suit to wear. It was oddly well fitting. Looking like a star in the provided suit, he joined his company in the living area. "Are you going to be joining Mr. King as well for dinner?" he asked curiously, already suspecting the answer he would receive by the way she was dressed.

"Yes, he has also invited me. You are under my watch and I wouldn't be doing my job properly if I was not there."

"Well, you look very nice, Miss Kale."

"Let's go!" demanded Amy as she turned for the door trying to hide the fact that the compliment made her blush slightly.

Outside sat a pickup truck rather than the usual mode of transportation. It was left running. Inside the cab it was warm. The evening was, so far, a nice treat with the abundance of heat Wes was able to soak in. He didn't realize how much he really had back home in the real world until it was all taken away from him and he was cast away into this horrid place.

They traveled down a road leading them even further from the town. The storm had died down and everything was covered in a fresh blanket of white as they continued towards their destination. No conversation was made as they drove. Rounding a final bend in the road, they arrived at a gated driveway. Amy hit a button on a little remote that was fastened on the sun visor and the large gothic styled gate slowly began to open, welcoming the presence of guests.

The driveway wound its way through the trees for a couple hundred yards before a house of unimaginable size became visible. The architecture was incredible. Although it appeared to be modern much of the style was taken from centuries in the past. The truck came to a stop in front of the main entrance where two stone lions sat guard at the bottom of the front steps that led to double, oversized doors that opened into the interior of the mansion.

Ascending the steps together, Wes and Amy entered through the front doors. The sheer beauty of the room took Wes's breath away. It was as if he had just walked into a palace ballroom. The focal points of the area consisted of a grand piano and a marble staircase that led to the upper floor. Even the smallest details were taken care of from the intricately carved animal faces in the bottom posts of the stairway's railings to the finely shaped decorative tiles that covered the ceiling.

"Wow, this place is amazing" were the only words Wes was able to muster as he watched the King descend the luxurious staircase dressed in very lavish attire.

"Welcome to my home, Mr. Petersen" proclaimed the King as he stepped down from the final stair.

"It must have cost you millions to build."

"A little over twelve" retorted the King smugly. "Please follow me into the dining room. The cook has prepared something special for us this evening."

"Twelve million?"

"That is what I said. I have to spend my money on something, don't I?" informed the King as he led his guests down a hallway.

Wes looked at Amy, catching her staring at him. Quickly she turned her gaze away. At the end of the hallway the King stopped in front of a large door. "In here." he directed.

Entering the room first, Wes found it to be just as extravagantly designed as the first room he had been privileged to see. He held the door open for the others to follow him in. A table big enough for twenty stood in the center of the room, its wooden surface polished so it gleamed in the light that flowed from the crystal chandelier that hung above it.

"Please take a seat" instructed the King as he took his own place at the head of the table. Amy sat to his right and Wes sat to his left.

"What do you think of my home, Mr. Petersen?"

"I think that you must have quite the profitable business going on here for you to be able to afford something so spectacular." Wes replied, trying to restrain himself from saying something he might regret in regards to the evil that supplied the funds to create such a place.

"That I do. Nuclear power is on the rise and uranium value is only going to increase, not to mention the money I bring in for making people vanish from regular society" voiced the King as he gave a slight chuckle. "Oh excellent, our food has arrived!" cheered the King as a man who Wes assumed played the role of a butler carried a silver platter into the room and placed it on the table. "My chef is one of the top chefs in the world. I had him brought here all the way from France. I hope you enjoy venison."

"I can't say that I've tried it before."

"Well then, you're in for a treat. Venison is Mr. King's favorite" piped up Amy as she reached over and stuck her fork into a large chunk of meat, placing it on her plate.

"Miss Kale is right, it is my favorite" acknowledged the King as he waved away the butler.

Wes noted that the butler never actually left the room. He went and stood in the corner, hidden by the shadows, awaiting any further commands. Taking full advantage of the meal, Wes loaded up his plate with an assortment of gourmet foods.

"So, Mr. Petersen, I am grateful for your help in catching that thief today. I have a feeling you could be of more use to me. Of course, if you help me, I will help you. Do you like that little house I have given you for the night?" the King inquired as he shovelled a fork full of mashed potatoes into his mouth.

"I do."

"Then maybe if you do as I say, we can make that your new permanent residence. What do you say, will you help me?"

Wes was unsure how to answer the King's inquiry. He did not want to help this monster. The man was evil, he had that poor kid killed less than two hours before and he was eating dinner without a care in the world. Looking to

Amy for some kind of help in how to answer, she gave him a quick nod indicating he should agree to the proposal presented to him. Who was she though? She was one of his employees, could he trust her direction? Figuring that at the very least, it would put him closer to the King which meant that Abhorson could possibly follow through on his promise, he replied to the question. "Yes, I will help you."

"Wonderful" exclaimed the King, clapping his hands together in excitement. "I will have Miss Kale bring you instructions tomorrow as to what I will need you to do as your first assignment. Remember, the more you do for me, the more comfortable I will make your life here. Just don't cross me in any way or you may end up like poor little Billy."

"What have I gotten myself into?" he thought to himself as the King's warning registered in his mind but he was unable to come up with an answer. "I will eagerly wait for your direction, Mr. King." he said, trying to remain optimistic about the coming days, although he feared his actions may eventually result in the death of another, if not himself.

"Good, good… Well, I am stuffed. Thank you for the company this evening." the King said as he stood up rubbing his bulging stomach. "Miss Kale will return you back to the executive suite for the night." Then without another word, the King left the room, leaving Amy and Wes alone.

"Are you ready to go?" asked Amy.

"Whenever you are."

"I am good to go now." she replied, rising from her chair.

"OK." Wes rose from his own chair heading for the exit a few paces behind Amy. As soon as they had stepped away from the table the butler jumped into action, beginning to clear the dirtied dishes that were left behind. The drive back to the little house seemed short. With a little coaxing he was able to get his companion to talk, even if it was just meaningless jabber about nothing in particular, it was a step closer to possibly having a friend on the inside. Climbing out of the truck he headed for the warmth of the dwelling, even considering a second hot bath to kick back and relax in. As he went inside he turned to close the door behind him and realized Amy had followed him up the path. Stepping to the side he allowed her space to enter the dwelling but she remained on the front step, the wind toying with her hair.

"Are you coming in?" he asked, curious as to why she had come up to the front porch.

"No, I just wanted to ask if you had everything you needed."

"Well, no. What I need is to go home but I don't think you can help me with that."

"You're right about that… Well, I'd best be going" Amy said as she turned around to head back down the walkway to her truck. Then, as a final thought, she called back up the path to him. "Good night, Wes." It was the first time she had called him by his first name.

Closing the door to the outside world, a clock on the wall informed him that it was nearly two in the morning but with everything that had been going on there was no way he was going to be able to get any sleep. There was just too much to think about.

Into the bathroom he went to draw himself another bath. He climbed in before it had finished filling, letting the water rise up against him. Leaving the massaging nature of the jets turned off, he just sat and thought. He thought about his deal with the King, he thought about Abhorson's promise, he thought about going home to his city apartment and, last but not least, he thought about Amy.

Chapter 4

Awakened by a knock on the front door Wes rose from his bed, stretching his arms as he crossed the house to answer the beckoning of the knock. Opening the door he was greeted by a guard he had not yet had the pleasure of meeting.

"Good morning, Mr. Petersen. I have your breakfast for you."

Wes stared at the man blindly for a moment before allowing him to step inside with the platter he was carrying. "Um, just set it on the table over there" he instructed, pointing towards the table in the kitchen area. Then he watched as the guard crossed the room, doing as he was told. It was an odd feeling to have one of the guards listen to his command. Under normal circumstances if he spoke that way to one of the King's employees there would be major hell to pay.

"Enjoy" stated the guard as he removed the lid on the platter and proceeded to exit the premises.

Wes thanked the man as he left. After closing the door behind him he went over to the table to see what kind of meal he would be supplied with for his supposed good behaviour. On the plate were two fried eggs and a steak, not just any steak though, it was a T-bone and happened to be cooked just the way he liked it. His mouth began to water just looking at the delicious piece of meat before him however, in the midst of eating the juicy perfectly cooked steak, he realized something. He was now truly alone, not in the sense that no one was in the house with him, but in the fact that he had no one he could trust. Abhorson had an agenda, the King was crazy, and although he was beginning to become fond of Amy, in the end she was still under the King's control.

After Wes was done eating he decided to head down to the library to check the book and see if his friend in the mask had left him another message, only the house was a little ways from town. Amy had brought him out and he was left without any mode of transportation other than walking, which would prove difficult in the snow that had accumulated during the storm.

Considering his options of walking or waiting for Amy to return, Wes opted for walking. It was cold but the sun was shining, allowing a walk back to town to potentially be nice. Trudging through the snow as the sun bounced off the glistening shine that yesterday's fresh layer of white stuff had produced made him long for a pair of sun glasses. Using his hand to shade his eyes he made good time getting to the library. He even stopped to admire a big bull moose that had been standing alongside the road for a few minutes.

The lights inside the library were turned off but he found the door to be unlocked just like the night before. Entering, Wes found the light switch right beside the entrance. The lights flickered on as he hit the switch with his palm. The room was just as he had left it the night before. Then again, why would it be any different? Going to the desk drawer he withdrew the black book. There was no new entry from his correspondent. Disappointed, he put the book back in its place. Just as he started to walk away though, he had an idea. What if he wrote a note to the masked person?

So, with that thought, Wes returned to the desk and withdrew the book once again and flipped it open to the next blank page. Searching the other desk drawers he was able to procure himself a pen. He knew exactly what he wanted to write.

> *Dear Friend*
>
> *I do not know who you are or why you're helping me or, for that matter, if I can even trust you. I know that that boy died last night as a result of my actions and I am very sorry for that. I am unsure what I should do next. What do you think my course of action should be?*

Upon completion of his note he returned the book to its resting place.

Taking a seat at the back table Wes continued reading the book about vampires he had started the evening before. After trying to focus on it for a while he finally gave up. There was too much going on in his head to get involved in some fictional story about blood sucking immortals.

Weighing his options of what to do with the rest of the day he decided to walk back to the house. He did not want to risk going any further into town when the majority of the population probably thought him to be some sort of snitch.

About halfway up the road heading back to the little house Wes heard the purr of an engine pulling up behind him. Turning around, he was surprised to see that it was Amy in the same truck she had been driving the night before. Rolling down her window, she called to him.

"Wes!"

"Yes?" he responded as he approached the side of her truck.

"I was just driving up to deliver you some lunch. Would you like a ride back up to the house?" offered Amy.

"Um, sure, I guess." he responded as he moved around to the passenger side of the vehicle and climbed in.

It only took a couple of minutes for them to arrive. Wes got out and headed inside. Amy followed behind him carrying his lunch. Setting the platter on the table she removed the lid. It was a feast if there ever was one, more than he could ever eat by himself.

"Care to join me for lunch? There is no way I could eat all that myself." he offered.

"I thought you would never ask" replied Amy with glee as she took a seat at the table and began to serve herself a healthy helping of different meats and cheeses that lay spread across the tray.

"This food is wonderful compared to what I have experienced so far at the dining hall" retorted Wes as he stuffed his mouth full of some sort of delicious sausage.

"Well, if you follow the King's instructions, then you can eat like this every day."

Wes froze. He no longer wanted Amy's company. With her comment he knew that her joining him was all some sort of a ploy to get him to become a spy for the King. Although he had agreed to it the night before he was still undecided on what exactly he should do. An answer to his note from the masked person may help sway him one way or the other, but who knew when or if that person would reply. "Please leave, Amy" Wes tried to say as calmly as possible, hoping to hide his disgust with her.

"What? Did I do something wrong?"

"Did you do something wrong you ask? How can you have the nerve to come in here and try to sway me into doing Mr. King's dirty deeds? It is wrong!!!" he said as his voice began to rise with anger, angry more at himself than anything for letting his guard down.

"How can you say that?" Amy stuttered, taken aback by Wes's outburst. "I am just trying to help you." Amy rose from the table and headed for the door. Opening it, she turned back to face Wes. "You're not the only one stuck in this hell hole, Wes!" she yelled, her voice cracking as she walked out slamming the door behind her.

Wes sat at the table, the silence of the room hurt. Had he misjudged Amy's intentions and insulted her? Maybe she was looking out for his best interests. Why did everything have to be so complicated? He did not know who he could trust anymore and it was starting to eat away at him.

No longer having an appetite he tossed what was left of the lunch into the garbage. He then began to pace back and forth across the room as he attempted to figure out what Amy's true intentions were. Out of nowhere her words pierced him like a knife. What did she mean when she said he wasn't the only one stuck here? Of course there were other prisoners, but she was a guard and what she said appeared to have had meaning to her in particular.

As frustration boiled in Wes's soul, he decided that leaving the house was what he needed to do. Without a ride he would be forced to walk to town once again. Suiting up in his winter gear he wandered out the door. As he turned back to close it he noticed an envelope taped to the outside. On the front it read "Instructions". Wes did not want to open it so he stuffed it into his pocket as he began his journey back to town.

The first stop on Wes's list was the library as he hoped his friend in the mask had returned, replying to the note he had left behind. Approaching the desk he took notice of the drawer he had left the book in. It was open slightly. He was positive he had closed it completely when he had placed the book there before. The masked individual must have returned, he thought to himself.

The book was definitely moved from where he had positioned it in the drawer but to his surprise there was no addition to its pages. For some reason his correspondent had not replied to his questions. Wes wondered if his correspondent knew about his deal with the King and was disappointed in his decision to agree to take on the King's tasks? Swearing under his breath he returned the book to its spot in the desk.

What to do next was the question going through his mind. He needed to return to the apartment but he had to be careful as he crossed the town. Who knew who could be lurking in the shadows, plotting some sort of revenge against him over Billy's hanging? He figured there was no good time to go since everyone knew who he was. He left the library, crossing the town square on route to his flat, hoping that Jack would have some advice for him. His attention was caught by the body hung up for all to see, swaying in the wind. The King was keeping his word about leaving Billy hung up as a reminder. It sent a chill down his spine and his thoughts then shifted to the envelope in his pocket. What evil did it contain?

Ignoring the urge to stop in his tracks and read the directions the King set out for him, he continued on his way when another thought hit him. There was a chance that Jack could be after him as well. It was a risk he had to take though, as he had no one else to turn to for help.

Something did not feel right as Wes entered the flat he and Jack had shared but he could not place a finger on what was causing the feeling. Jack was seated just as he had been the first time they had met, feet perched on the window sill and smoke rising from the end of the pipe that drooped lazily from the corner of his mouth.

Cautiously, he moved further into the room. "Jack?" he said, tossing a little bait out to see how Jack would respond to his presence.

"Ah Wes, you have returned." replied Jack as he spun his chair around to face him. "You know, Wes, I think you're a good guy so it is a bit of a shame that I have to allow this to happen."

"Allow what to happen?"

"This."

Wes countered Jack's comment with a blank stare then it hit him, literally. Someone had walked into the room behind him while he was speaking with Jack and clubbed him over the head with a bat.

Vision faded as his knees collapsed under the weight of his body. He lost consciousness without ever being able to see his attackers face. The last image in his mind was Jack removing the pipe from his mouth about to say something, to who he was unsure.

***

Wes's vision slowly returned. His head was cloudy as to what had happened before everything went black. A pain throbbed on the back of his head. Voices were incoherent around him as others in the room talked but he slowly began to make sense of the conversation taking place in the room around him.

"He has been out a long time." one said right before another replied, "Shut up, he is coming to!"

Wes went to place his hand where he had been hit but his arms were tied behind the back of his chair. Trying to stand up he found that his legs were also bound in place by a length of rope. As his sight began to clear, a face became apparent in front of him. It was Abhorson; he sat on a stool staring at Wes as his captive's senses slowly returned.

"Hello Wes, it is a pleasure to see you again" chuckled Abhorson as he stood up from the stool. "We need to discuss some things." Walking out of Wes's sight, Abhorson continued to speak. "Firstly, I want to apologize for the little bump to the head but I could not let you know where our hideout is. Secondly, I understand that the plan is going along well. You are moving towards the King's circle of trust. We do have a little problem though. Have you read your letter with the instructions from the King yet?" asked Abhorson as he came back into view.

Wes gazed around the room trying to figure out where he was. The air was thick and smoky, the wall made of wood paneling. They could be anywhere in the prison's confines. On the wall, assortments of guns were displayed. "Um, no! I have not read it yet." Wes answered after sitting for a moment taking in the sights while Abhorson's words slowly took shape in his mind.

"Well, why don't I read it to you!" piped up another voice from behind him. It sounded very similar to Jack's. "Hello Wes," he said as he moved into his field of vision. The letter was in his hand and he began to read. "Wes, my task for you is very simple. I need you to get rid of your roommate Jack. The local doctor has informed me that Jack has cancer. The doctor is the Asian man that you ran into the other day when you were returning home. Due to the high cost of treatment, especially in an area as remote as this, it is more cost effective to have Jack removed from the equation. Please inform me once your task is complete."

"What do you think of that, Wes? Do you have the balls to get rid of me?" Jack snarled.

Now Alert, Wes did not know what to say. "Um, well, ah."

"You should be answering 'YES', Wes! My life is worth the sacrifice in order to get this operation off the ground. You are the key player here. Without you, we cannot end the King's reign of terror." stated Jack

Taking over the talking Abhorson spoke up. "We have a plan, Wes. Jack is going to remain hidden. He has stocked up on extra pills so that he won't run out of medication for a while. You must return to the King tomorrow to inform him that you have dealt with your task. Can you do that?"

"Yes" he replied, still astonished that Jack was working with Abhorson all along. How many others were there involved?

"Good. I hope that next time we do not have to use force when we want to speak to you, but as of yet we do not know if you can be trusted. I hope you understand this. However, if you continue doing well by us then we may be able to let you in on some of our secrets. As well, I will be able to get you home." Abhorson removed a large syringe from his coat pocket. "This will knock you out, but I promise that you will wake up in your bed safely."

Abhorson then handed the syringe to the Asian doctor who now walked into view.

"This will only hurt but a bit" said the Asian man as he rolled up Wes's sleeve and plunged the needle into his arm making Wes wince in pain. "You have about ninety seconds before you're out cold."

Abhorson began to speak again as Wes slowly felt himself slipping into darkness. "Do not go to the mines tomorrow. You must go directly to the King in the morning, informing him of Jack's demise."

Wes heard Abhorson's words but as the man finished his sentence he could no longer make out what was being said. The only thing Wes could coherently understand was laughter between some of the men in the room then it was all gone. He was sent away into his own little world where nothing but darkness existed. In this land of nothing, dreams did not come to rescue him. He remained thoughtless until the point at which he would be awakened.

Chapter 5

Wes awoke with a migraine. His head hurt severely, as if he had been out drinking heavily the night before only he remembered everything that had happened, or at least what he had been conscious for. He was unsure whether the headache was a result of the drugs or the blow to the head but he stumbled to the kitchen where he had seen a bottle of Tylenol on the counter the night he had arrived. To his luck it was still sitting there untouched from before. Tossing a couple pills back and rinsing them down with water from the tap he then proceeded to the washroom to take a shower. At that point the numbing sensation of the cold water would be beneficial to his aches.

The icy flow of water ran down his body, its touch washing off some of the horror that occurred the night before. Once finished he got dressed in another set of clean clothing that had been left behind by his predecessor. He wondered where he could get his dirty clothes washed and decided he would try to check into it at some point later in the day.

After getting ready, Wes debated with himself whether he should go for something to eat or go directly to the King to inform him the task was done. Throwing a glance towards the clock on the wall it dawned on him that it was already lunch time. He had no idea how long he had slept or what the consequences of missing his shift at the mine might result in. Weighing his options, he decided it would be better to deal with the King first as he would be taking his life in his own hands if he dared to walk into the dining hall when Billy's body still swung in the wind of the town square just outside the hall as a constant reminder to the other inhabitants of the prison that he was a traitor to them all.

Figuring the King would be at his office this time in the day he headed in that direction. As he walked he wondered if he would run into Amy. He longed for the chance to apologize for insulting her, even if he could not yet trust her. At least he enjoyed her company. Compared to the previous days, the weather was considerably nicer. Although still crisp, the cold's attempt at nipping his skin failed due to the armor of winter gear he had come into possession of since arriving.

A fear grew in him as he approached the building that housed the King's office. There were an outrageous number of guards surrounding the premises, all of whom were armed with rifles, ready to shoot any potential threat. Coming up to the front doors a guard stepped in the way blocking his passage into the foyer.

"What is your business here, prisoner?"

"Mr. King is expecting me."

"Is that so?" asked the guard as he mumbled into a little hand held radio. There was static on the other end before a voice answered the call. He could not understand what was being said through the radios interference but the guard stepped to the side allowing him to gain entry into the building.

The hallway was empty; there were no souls to be seen. Wes remembered which office belonged to the King though. How could he forget? He had lost all hope in that office only a couple days prior. Knocking on the glass pane, the King answered from inside "Come in" and Wes stepped through the door. "Ah, hello Mr. Petersen. Should you not be out at one of the mines right now?"

"I thought it was more important that I relay the fact to you that the Jack issue has been dealt with."

"That is excellent to hear. I am surprised at how swiftly you were able to carry out your task…and to think Miss Kale didn't believe you would have the guts to deal with the problem." said the King chuckling to himself. I guess I owe you another night in the executive suite."

"What do you mean another night? I thought it was going to be a permanent place for me."

"Well, I guess you should have attended work, Mr. Petersen. Just because we have a little side thing going on here doesn't mean that you can break the rules. Although, because of our little thing going on, I won't follow through with the typical consequence that missing work would invoke."

Wes turned around and stormed out of the office. He was angry. Sure, he didn't really do the task he was assigned, but the King was manipulative. He had a suspicion that if he had gone to the mine and not gone to the King at once he would have lost out on the house for the exact opposite reason that he did.

A frustrated Wes plodded his way over to the library praying for an answer from his secret masked helper. The lights inside were on and he was a little fuzzy about whether or not he had remembered to turn them off the night before. Just like the previous time he checked, the black book had no new entries. As he stood running his eyes over the empty page he had hoped to find filled, he heard movement in the back of the room behind the aisles of reading material.

Moving very slowly, he crept his way towards the back where the table and chairs were located. Upon reaching the last aisle, he ducked down to hide. In order to gain a view of the area he removed a couple books off the shelf, trying to not make a sound as he peered through the opening he had just created. Sitting there undisturbed was Amy. He watched her, noticing that she was an extraordinarily beautiful woman. He just never really realized it previously. It was almost serene to just sit and watch her read.

"Are you going to just keep sitting back there being a creep?" Amy asked looking up from her book, her question catching him by surprise. "I know it's you, Wes. I can see your reflection in the mirror on the wall."

Accepting that he had been caught he stepped out from behind the shelving wearing an expression of embarrassment. "Hey!" he exclaimed. "I am just browsing the book selection" he informed her as he tried to give a plausible reason for being where he was. "I did want to talk to you, though. I am sorry about yesterday."

"It's okay, Wes. I understand it is hard to trust anyone here, including me."

"It is" he said, a small grin appearing on his face.

"Wes, I want to show you something. Will you come with me?"

"Sure, I guess."

"Great," Amy replied as she closed the book she was reading. "Let's go."

Following, he was led outside and around to the back of the building where Amy had stashed her snowmobile. She placed a helmet on her head but did not have a spare one for Wes so he went without.

"Hold on tight" called Amy as she took off with him riding on the back. He did not have the faintest idea where she was taking him.

"Where are we going?" he yelled, but his voice was left unheard, drowned out by the roar of the engine.

For nearly thirty minutes they rode without slowing down until they came to a small log cabin set on a hill overlooking Lake Athabasca. The view was magnificent. Living in the city, Wes had never had much opportunity to venture out into nature. This became one of the most beautiful views to have graced his eyes.

Jumping off the back of the sled, he walked up to the front porch of the cabin. On it was a swinging bench hung from the rafters. He sat down, gazing out over the hillside. Amy removed her helmet, setting it down and taking a seat beside him on the bench. Down below was a field of snow that led up to the lakeside. Several deer were frolicking around it as if they were taking part in nature's ballet for their audience of two.

"This place is amazing" Wes whispered into Amy's ear as he placed his arm around her. At that moment he did not care if he could trust her or not. It was just such a wonderful experience that he wanted to share it with her no matter her true intentions.

"Thank you. This is where I like to come to think." Amy whispered back as she made eye contact with her guest. "Can I ask you something?"

"Sure."

"Did you really kill Jack?"

Oh no, thought Wes. He did not want the moment to end. This could be a test. If he told the truth she could report back to the King, but if he lied there was the chance that she would hate him for it. He just wanted to remain in the peaceful realm where he had just been residing but time could not be frozen. He had to answer. Taking his chances he told the truth, "No, I did not kill Jack. I am not a killer."

"Oh, that is wonderful." Amy said while her eyes lit up with respect. She saw a glimmer of worry in his eyes though so she made an attempt to extinguish his fear. "Don't worry. It will stay between you and me."

Even though Amy's words reduced his level of worry, it did not all fade. He was still not sure he could trust her completely. She could still be operating under some plan the King had devised. It would be evil to toy with someone like that but as the King had demonstrated with Billy, there were no boundaries that he would not dare to cross.

"Now, can I ask you something?" spoke Wes.

"What is it you want to know?"

"When you left during lunch…what did you mean when you said that I was not the only one trapped here? It seemed like it had meaning directly related to you when you said it."

"It is not just the prisoners that are stuck here. Mr. King will not allow me to leave, or any of the guards for that matter. It is part of the agreement upon signing up. He finds people down on their luck and offers them a job, a place to live, and good food. Providing that the rules are followed, life is not bad as a guard. The only problem is that once the contract is signed, Mr. King essentially owns the signee's soul."

"Oh, wow. I am so sorry, I didn't realize that you are just as much a prisoner as I am." he said, a bit of pity in his voice.

"Don't feel bad, I have accepted my fate. Now forget about this ugly topic. This place is supposed to be happy. I don't want you ruining it." Amy teased as she jabbed him in the ribs in a playful fashion.

"Ouch."

"You big baby!"

Amy then rested her head on her companion's shoulder. They sat silent as they watched the sun go down over the frozen lake. Once darkness fell, the northern lights began to waltz across the sky to the tune of a wolf howling somewhere in the distance. Without moving, she remained embraced in his arms for nearly two hours before he finally spoke up. "We should probably be getting back now."

"You're right. Let me get you back. I will drop you off at the executive suite. Since you have it for the night again, I am sure that you probably want to make good use of the hot water."

"I wouldn't mind putting it to use" laughed Wes. "Cold showers are pretty horrible in the middle of winter."

"I can imagine."

Getting up, he and Amy returned to the snowmobile to begin their journey back to town. He felt like he had achieved a win for the first time since arriving at Uranium City, even if it was only for an evening. During his time with Amy sitting on the front porch of that old cabin with her in his arms, he had almost forgotten where he really was.

Amy took him straight to the little house. She even walked up the path with him. When they arrived at the door she spoke, "I had a really nice time tonight."

"So did I." he responded as he opened the door to go inside.

"Then you won't mind if I do this," she said as she leaned in planting a quick kiss on his lips. It was short but he could feel the spark between them. Just as unexpectedly as she had kissed him she turned around and bolted down the path. Wes was left standing at the front door, caught somewhere between utter shock and an overabundance of glee.

When Wes's mind caught up to what had just transpired, Amy was already gone, leaving him with nothing left to do except enter the house. The room was dark so he reached for the light switch which instantly cast light throughout the living room area and kitchen.

"Why, hello again, Wes." said Abhorson who was seated at the kitchen table, his cane hooked on the back of a second chair that sat to his right.

Wes looked at him with utter shock and surprise. The evening's magic had now come to an end. After all, this was Uranium City Prison, a place where fairy tale endings did not exist. "Abhorson…what are you doing here?"

"I came to ask something of you," the old man said as he grabbed his cane, using it to help himself stand up, "but when I arrived you were not here." He took a step towards Wes. "You were off gallivanting with that guard woman." He took another step. "Do you know the consequences for socializing with a guard?" One more step and Abhorson stood at arm's length from him. "You remain silent, which gives me the impression that you do know how severe they are," Abhorson took his cane, swinging it at the back of Wes's knee.

Wes cursed in pain as his leg gave out from under him caused by the powerful blow of the man's attack. Falling to the floor he looked up at the old man before him. Choosing to remain silent, he waited for Abhorson to speak again.

"You could have ruined everything. This is not about you; this is about the good of us all. I forbid you to have any contact with her again." Abhorson stepped towards the door, opening it to allow his exit. "One last thing…tomorrow a man is going to try and kill you. It is not staged so be prepared to defend yourself. It is imperative that you survive."

Slamming the door as he left the house, the old man was gone. Wes still lay on the floor, a large bruise already developing on the back of his leg where the cane had struck him. Fear was building inside, he had no doubt that his life was in danger. If he had learned anything thus far it was that the people in this place were ruthless.

Getting into a standing position he limped over to the kitchen to remove a bottle of water from the fridge. He sat down at the table to drink it while he tried to devise a plan for keeping himself alive the following day. Nothing was coming to him though, so he decided to retreat to a hot bath where at least the soothing waters would help to relieve the new found pain in his leg.

After the comfort of the bath he made his way to the bedroom, remembering to set the alarm. He would attend his shift at the mine tomorrow. If he went about his normal day he hopefully wouldn't tip off his assailant, therefore he would at least have the upper hand knowing an attack would be coming.

Chapter 6

Sleep evaded Wes during the night. The pain in his leg held him from the sweet sanctum that his dreams could offer, however the swelling from where he had been hit over the head had receded. Throughout the sleepless night he had thought about the day to come. He still had yet to devise a concrete plan on how he was going to save his own life. All he would be able to do was watch everyone around him for hints of the attack that was to come. No one could be ruled out as a non-threat.

Turning the alarm off before it ever got the chance to scream out, Wes rose from bed. Bags had appeared under his eyes from the lack of sleep. He had to leave slightly earlier than normal in order to make it to the dining hall for a meal before work since the house was located a larger distance away than the apartment.

On top of the pain that shot up through his body with every step, his stomach groaned in anticipation for food. To say he was nervous would be an understatement of the feelings he had about going to the dining hall. He had not dared to enter it since he was framed for ratting out Billy to the King, which had ultimately resulted in the boy's death. If someone were to attack him there, he was sure no one would bother to reach out and help him. Everyone would probably cheer on the attacker as he was strangled, or knifed, or beaten to a bloody death.

The walk took a long time due to his recent injury. He wondered how much damage had really been done to his leg from the blow Abhorson had laid upon him. Stumbling into the dining hall, everyone's eyes shifted towards him and they were all still overflowing with hatred. It could be felt in the glaring eyes that were cast his way. Wes came to the conclusion that there was no going back. He would forever be an outcast. His only hopes were divided between the masked individual and Abhorson's promise. Both options were not good bets but what else could he do?

On this morning, there were no empty tables. People seemed to be spread out, with two people at some tables and three at others. After Wes got his food he took a seat at a table where two others were seated. As soon as he sat down the men glared at him for having the guts to sit down at their table. Ignoring their looks of annoyance he began to eat. The two men quickly stood up, picking up their trays of food and making their way across the room to relocate to another table to finish their meals.

Alone at a table once again, he ate his food in silence. All around him he could feel the eyes of the other prisoners staring in his direction. As he finished his meal he slowly slipped the knife that came with his breakfast into his pocket. He knew he was being watched and he held hope that it would scare off any potential confrontations with the other prisoners. His only worry was that whoever was supposed to take him out that day had seen him take the knife, for if they had it wouldn't be much use as they would have prepared for his actions of defense.

On the bus the situation was the same, there were just enough seats to accommodate everyone but, rather than sitting down beside Wes, one guy insisted on standing in the aisle the entire trip to the mine.

The morning went by smoothly in the sense that no one tried to kill him. The men came and collected their tags, only acknowledging him because it was a requirement of their job to do so. It was at the end of the day when things started to go awry. Two of the miners never returned their tags at the end of their shift so, after waiting a few extra minutes to see if they were just running behind, he trudged through the snow over to the safety shack to inform Arnold Dunn of the missing men.

Dunn was seated at his desk inside the building. "What can I do for you, Mr. Petersen?" he asked with surprise when he saw Wes enter the room.

"Two of the men never came out of the mine today."

"Oh, well now, that is no good." Arnold stroked his chin. It was a funny gesture as he had no facial hair, which was typically a characteristic of someone who would be found doing such an act. "I suppose you should go into the mine and find them."

"Me?" asked Wes in shock. "But, I have never been in the mine. I don't know where to look, not to mention that I have to catch the bus back into town."

"Too bad, Mr. Petersen, I am promoting you to search and rescue. When you come back out, I will give you a ride back to town in my truck."

"But…"

"No buts! Go do it and don't come back until you have found them." Mr. Dunn ordered, raising his voice to suppress Wes's objections.

So much for surviving the day, Wes thought to himself as he headed for the mine. Just inside the entrance he found a flashlight on a poorly constructed shelf. When the switch failed to turn it on he hit the light in his palm a few times and brought the bulb to life. The main tunnel was well lit, but some of the tunnels that went off to the sides were dark and gloomy. He flashed the light down those ones as he passed, making his way deeper into the bowls of the mine.

A chill ran up his spine. Something wasn't right about this situation. Why didn't the miners come up to the surface? If some sort of gas had gotten to them, this was a suicide mission, then again if they were trapped by a cave-in he could be a hero. His task had the potential of regaining some trust with the other prisoners so he pushed himself to go further into the depths of the mine.

Rounding a corner Wes saw the two men lying on the ground. They were not moving. No longer thinking about the risk of deadly gases, he rushed to their sides to see if they were still breathing.

Upon inspection of the bodies he found their necks were broken. The realization that this was some sort of ploy to get him alone in the mine struck him. Half expecting to turn around and find someone waiting to strike him down, he turned back to look at the path behind him. To his surprise, he did not find some axe wielding murderer ready to pounce on him like in some scary movie. It was just as it was when he walked through the corridor a minute before, empty of living souls.

Wes had to get out of the mine. He began to sprint up the path towards the surface, leaving the flashlight lying beside the bodies of the dead prisoners. He reached the entrance out of breath and gasping for air from the sudden bout of cardio he had forced upon himself. A cramp had developed in his stomach and his leg raged in pain from the exertion it had just been put through.

Looking out into the equipment yard, he found that it had started to snow at a heavy pace. Already the accumulation had progressed to over two inches of the white stuff. Out of fear, he drove himself forward towards Arnold Dunn's office, his leg growing worse with every stride.

"Mr. Dunn, someone killed the men!" he yelled as he came crashing through the front door of the safety shack.

Arnold Dunn was seated in his office chair with his back to the entrance, not responding in any way to Wes's sudden entry. Approaching the silent Mr. Dunn, Wes reached out and pushed the chair with his had to spin it around.

The chair spun revealing a sight that was beyond gruesome. Someone had slit the throat of Arnold Dunn. His face was pale, drained of all blood. Wes had been in such a hurry upon entering that he had failed to notice the pool of blood on the floor around the office chair. Dunn's shirt was soaked in red and a note was stapled to his chest. Its writing looked as if it had been scribbled out by a preschooler. It only contained two words; they were "Wes Petersen."

Three more men had now died because of him and he feared he would be next. He had no way to return to town for help, he had to find somewhere to hide until the bus returned with the night shift crew. But where could he hide? And what if he ran into the killer while he was looking for a hiding place?

His second question was answered almost immediately as a large man stepped through the front door of the shack. Wes retreated to behind the body of Arnold Dunn. The man who had just entered the room stood over six and a half feet tall and was nearly just as big around. When he saw Wes, a large toothless grin became apparent on the man. A tattoo of a Chinese symbol hugged his bald scalp.

"Wes Petersen, I gonna gech you!!" stated the man, his speech resembling that of a mentally challenged individual.

Although Wes could tell the man had a disability immediately after he spoke, he could also tell that the giant man was very powerful in strength. Attempting to reason with the large man, he spoke to him. "Let's talk this through, big fella. You don't have to kill me." As he spoke, he cautiously reached into his pocket to extract the knife he had stashed. To his surprise it was gone, lost somewhere in the snow as he had run across the yard site.

"I do what the boss say, I gech you!" cried the big man as he lunged forward towards his prey.

Wes saw the signs of what the man was about to do before he had a chance to make his attack. With quick reflexes, he pushed Dunn's office chair towards the big man. This resulted in a collision that sent both the assailant and Dunn's body crashing to the floor in a heap of blood and gore.

Taking the opportunity to escape while the attacker was attempting to regain a standing position, Wes darted out the door as fast as his crippled leg would allow him to go. Once outside, he considered his options. Option one…run and hide, the mine being the most obvious place to disappear in. Option two…go back inside and find the keys to the pickup that Dunn drove which would be an unintelligent move since the man inside would probably be up and on his feet by then. Or, option three, stand his ground and fight. This was another not so suitable option based on the sheer size of the attacker.

Going with option one, Wes continued his gimped run towards the mine entrance. It was his best bet for being able to survive but there was the possibility that he could get lost in the darkest corners of the mines intestines.

As he approached the mouth of the mine, he looked back through the snow towards the shack. The big man had regained his composure and was now barreling across the site towards him with the force of a train. Quickly, he limped into the mine and plunged himself deeper and deeper into its bowels, beyond the point where he had previously found the bodies of the two men a short while earlier. As he passed the flashlight he had left lying on the ground, he considered stopping to pick it up but in the brief seconds that he contemplated such an action he could hear the thunderous footsteps of the big man gaining on him. There was no time for anything. He needed to find somewhere to duck into before the man gained a visual on him. It would only be a matter of seconds, as he felt that his leg would not hold out much longer.

Coming upon a fork in the tunnel he had to choose which path to take, the left path being well lit, the right leading into a dark corridor. This was his final chance at survival and he dashed into the darkness just as the man behind him rounded the last bend in the tunnel that would have allowed him to spot his target.

Leaning against the tunnel wall a short way into the darkness, Wes did not have it in him to travel any further. The pain in his leg was becoming too much to bear. If he were to try and move on he felt that he may scream out in agony from every step he would try to take. All he could do was pray that the man chasing him would choose to go down the opposite corridor.

From inside the shadows, Wes could see the large man standing at the fork, contemplating his choices in direction. He felt like cheering when the man stepped towards the opposing tunnel. Shifting himself into what he thought would be a more comfortable position to wait out help, he accidently kicked a small stone that had been hidden by the darkness of the corridor. The noise from the rock bouncing along the floor echoed through the tunnels.

"This is the end" he whispered to himself when the man changed his course into the tunnel that harbored him in its darkness.

"I gech ya now!" hollered the beast who was there to end his life. The large man picked up a pickaxe which happened to be leaning against the wall where the fork in the paths existed. In two strides, the man had reached his victim's weakened body. He lifted the axe as if he was up to bat at a baseball game. Bracing himself for impact, Wes closed his eyes. He was too tired to try and fight anymore. Why prolong the inevitable? As the man swung the pickaxe, a gunshot rang out sending a bullet ripping through his chest and he began to collapse. Although the direction of the axe was altered, it was already in motion and clipped the side of Wes's head.

Immediately, Wes could feel the blood running down his face below where the pick axe struck him and he became light headed. His whole body wrenched in pain and he could feel himself slowly sliding down the tunnel wall to a sitting position as his legs buckled beneath him, his vision growing blurry with every inch closer to the ground that he got. He could still make out his attacker's body in front of him.

The large man was lying on his back, choking on his own blood as his lungs filled with the red fluid that kept him alive. A smile still resided on his face as he took his final choking gasp for air. The reality of the situation began to take hold of Wes, someone had shot the man who was about end his life. Looking in the direction of the lit area, he could see his guardian angel standing there, face covered in a ski mask and an old revolver in hand, barrel still smoking from its recent use.

Wes watched as the masked person tucked the gun into their belt before moving to his side. Reaching down to Wes, who was now completely sitting on the floor of the mine, the masked individual slowly helped him to his feet. His senses were tuning in and out as he was helped to stagger slowly to the outside world. Not a word was said between the two as they moved as one unit, Wes being unable to talk, the masked person simply not choosing to talk. His savior didn't even offer words of support, just ongoing silence.

Wes was slowly fading out. He assumed it was from blood loss, he could feel himself soaked in it. Things began to feel dream like to him as his body slowly drove itself into a complete state of shock. He knew that in shock amazing things could happen. He had once met someone who had broken their back in a car accident before getting out of the vehicle and walking around while the shock had a hold on the individual.

In the distance Wes could now make out snow. They were approaching the exit. The snow had piled up significantly since he had gone back into the mine in an attempt to save his own life. He had no idea how long he was in there. It felt like hours but must have only been a short time as the night shift had yet to arrive. There were no vehicles in the yard outside besides his former supervisor's pickup. Then, just as he made it a few feet out into the yard, blackness struck and he collapsed outside in the falling snow. With a final feat of strength he came back to reality long enough to see the bus carrying the night shift workers pull into the yard.

Someone came running over to him, calling out. He tried to call back but the effort sent him back into an unconsciousness state. He was out cold, left lying on the frigid ground as a group of men surrounded his motionless body.

Chapter 7

Assorted pains were coursing through every inch of Wes's body as he began to regain consciousness. Looking around, he had no idea where he was. The room was very white and extremely clean for something that would be found in Uranium City Prison. He then noticed the IV's hooked into his arms. This place was some sort of hospital room. Outside he could hear footsteps approaching the door; he decided to close his eyes, pretending to still be unconscious.

The Asian doctor opened the door, entering with the King at his side.

"When is he going to wake up, Dr. Cho?" asked the King, putting on a very transparent tone of concern.

"Anytime now, I hope. We were able to get him stabilized but he did lose a lot of blood. The last three days we have kept him sedated in order to keep things under control. He was very lucky to survive such a brutal attack." Checking Wes's vitals, the doctor continued to speak. "I took him off sedation this morning so it is only a matter of time before he awakens."

"Very good, Dr. Cho, let me know if there are any changes. I have big plans for this boy. Also, I have a few questions about the attack. I am hoping that with the answers, I can prevent such a thing from happening again" stated the King as he exited the room, leaving the doctor alone with his patient.

"You can open your eyes now. I know that you are conscious. Your breathing pattern changes from when you're sleeping to when you're awake."

"I feel funny," Wes said as he opened his eyes and began a fit of coughing.

"That would probably be due to the fact that you are very heavily drugged up on pain killers. You have a severely damaged knee, a compound fracture to your skull, and variety of other health issues from lack of eating and dehydration. As you heard me say to Mr. King, you are very lucky to be alive."

"You helped do this to me, you bastard!" a second fit of coughing hit Wes as he spoke.

"Hush now, Mr. Petersen. We don't want anyone to overhear our conversation. I need you to be a good little soldier. If you're going to compromise our operation, then maybe you could fall ill from an infection during one of the surgeries required by your wounds, slip into a coma and later die as a result. Mr. King would never question it. He knows my resources are not that great and he would never call anyone else in to check up on your death. His number one priority is to keep this place a secret from the public's eye."

"When can I get out of here?" Wes asked, dropping the previous subject. He had no doubt in his mind that the Asian doctor would follow through if he were to leak out the information of their revolt against the King.

"Tomorrow, if there are no complications that arise." answered the doctor as he began to leave the room. "I am going to go inform the King that you have awakened. I suggest you tell him what he wants to hear, making sure to leave out our involvement of course."

Wes nodded in response to the doctor's order, the small movement a strain on his condition. A debriefing with the King was something he did not look forward to. It was obvious that Dr. Cho had been able to catch up with the King before he had left as it was only a few minutes before the King entered the room to consult with him.

"I am glad to see that you have awakened, Mr. Petersen" said the King as he approached the side of his bed. "I want to ask you some questions regarding the other night." The King pulled over a stool, taking a seat on it. "Firstly, did you know the man that attacked you?"

"No." Wes replied weakly.

"Do you know why this man came after you?"

"No." he said again, lying.

"Well, I hate to say this, but I think you did a good job bringing down this man all by yourself" admitted the King.

Wes contemplated telling him that he had not been the one to bring down the beast of a man and then thought better of it, so he just remained silent and thought about the attack while the King spoke. Then a question crossed his mind, one that he did not dare ask out loud. How could the King think he killed his attacker when the man was brought down by a gun? Just as quick as the question came to mind, so did the answer. The King was never informed of the fact that the man was shot. Dr. Cho would have fed him some other story about cause of death and Abhorson would have made sure everything was covered up with a plausible story, leaving the great and powerful warden of the prison oblivious to the situation.

"When you are able to leave this place I want you to come to my office and see me. I think your talents are being wasted handing out tags at the mine and I would like to reassign you to a different position." The King stood up, walking over to the window to look out at the world he had created. "I also need to tell you something in confidence. I fear that the attack on you was because of me. It has come to my attention that a man has been able to enter the prison under a false identity; a man who has come here to kill me, Mr. Petersen. I believe that he thinks you to be a spy of some sort for me, and therefore sent someone to kill you." Turning back to face Wes, the King then asked "Do you know anything about this?"

"I don't know anything about that." he replied, once again lying.

"Okay, I will send Miss Kale by to check on you later. I think you may be able to help me with my little problem." the King stated as he exited the room, shutting the door behind him.

Thinking, Wes laid in the hospital bed in silence. Abhorson's plan was right on track. However, he was just a pawn in a game of chess being played between the two men. They were both aware that a game was in play but he was unsure how aware each of the men was to the other's next move. He needed to pick a side. He could no longer be neutral. The question was what side was in his best interest? Abhorson's...the man who had nearly killed him, but promised a way home? Or the King's...the man who could condemn a young boy to death without batting an eye and would never allow him to leave this horrid place.

The strain on his mind eventually wore him out and sleep took him away from the horrors that had become his life. Throughout the afternoon he slept, awaking briefly when Amy stopped in to check on him. He was unable to keep his eyes open long enough to hold a conversation so he was unsure how long she remained with him in the medical room but, when he awoke again, she was gone.

Darkness had taken the room. The little illumination that remained was a result of the moon casting its glow through the small window. Wes could hear footsteps in the hallway outside. The sound grew closer with each beat of the shoes on the floor. As they reached the exterior of the door they stopped. He had no idea who would be bothering him in what he assumed was the middle of the night. Time was unknown to him due to the lack of a clock in the room.

Slowly the door opened, squeaking on its hinges. In stepped the silhouette of a man. Wes immediately knew who his visitor was because of the cane in the silhouette's right hand that kept him sturdy. It was not footsteps he had been hearing, it was the banging of the cane on the floor as Abhorson moved forward towards his room. Another step closer allowed the moon's light to wash over the intruder's vacant eyes, their hollowness draining the very life from the already bleak room.

"I see that you survived, Wes." said Abhorson as he took a seat in the same place the King had sat earlier in the day. "I feel it is time to share a little truth with you."

"Is that so?" Wes asked weakly from his hospital bed.

"It is so. You being brought here was no mistake, Wes. It was intentional. We paid Scott a handsome sum of money to be gone the night you were taken so that you would be brought in his place. We needed it to seem like a mistake, allowing you to grow closer to Mr. King's circle of trust." Wes remained quiet while Abhorson shared this information but inside he was fuming at the revelation of this new information. "Now, I must tell you a story. In this story, you will understand why you were chosen to help end the King's reign." Clearing his throat, Abhorson began.

"Many years ago two men escaped from a prison that did not exist. They were the only ones who ever successfully escaped. The warden of the prison was angry for he had been duped. In order to get revenge he sent killers to slaughter the families of these men. The first of these two men had no family. He was a loner and his only friend was his partner who he escaped with. The second had a wife and a young son. In the middle of the night, the warden's minions entered the home of the young wife. She was slaughtered in cold blood however the son was not there." Abhorson briefly paused in the story he was telling to light a cigarette and the flame from his match danced across his hideous face as he lit the smoke. "The young boy who was not there had been staying at his grandparents the night of his mother's death. Is this starting to sound familiar?"

A tear rolled down Wes's face, the young boy in Abhorson's story was him. His mother had been murdered during a night while he was at his grandparents when he was just a toddler. The killers were never found. "The boy in the story is me?"

"Yes, the boy is you. Do you now see why you were chosen? I have granted you the ability to avenge your mother's death. I have had you watched for a long time now, studied your habits and learned your past. It is your fate that you are here today."

"What of my father?" asked Wes.

"That, I cannot answer. After the two men escaped no one ever heard from either of them again."

"So, you want me to kill the King?"

"No, I want you to help in ending the King's cruelty. I am not asking you to kill him, although you may want to since he was the reason behind your mother's death."

He knew that Abhorson was trying to plant the idea of killing the King in his head, it was working. He also knew that he was not capable of actually killing someone. He couldn't even kill a fish the summer before when he had gone fishing with Scott. "You are a real bastard. I nearly died because of you. Now, while I am lying here recuperating, you bring up my mother's death… Get out!" he ordered in an attempt at a yell but he was still too weak, the effort sending him into another fit of coughing.

Abhorson did as he was demanded. He rose from his seat, leaving the room without another word. Wes lay still in the bed listening to the rhythm of the cane thumping along the hallway until the sound had completely faded. Although he did not trust Abhorson, he believed him that the King was responsible for the death of Marie, his mother. Ultimately, he now knew which direction he would follow in the battle that was destined to come.

Chapter 8

In the morning Wes found himself in much better shape than he had been the day before. Most of the pain had subsided, complemented by an increase in energy. There were several things on his mental list of things to do for the day providing Dr. Cho allowed him to leave. First on his list was to visit the library to see if his masked friend had left him a note. Second he would go to the King's office as he had been instructed to do.

While he lay planning out his day, Amy entered the room. When she realized he was awake she immediately ran over to give him a hug.

"Ouch," yelped Wes as she wrapped her arms around him.

"Sorry. I was so worried that you wouldn't be alright." she said, releasing her grip on him. "I just talked to Dr. Cho and he says you are able to leave today but have to return this evening for one more night of observation."

"That's good, I feel like getting out and stretching my legs"

"Well, Mr. King wants to see you. I will walk over there with you."

"That would be good," Wes said with a slight smile appearing on his face. That meant he had to postpone the journey over to the library but it was okay because he would get to spend time with Amy. He hoped that when everything came to an end in this Hell he would be able to get Amy out of here as well.

Amy helped brace him as he climbed out of the bed. He was shaky on his feet after being stuck in a bed for the previous few days. It also did not help that the injury to his leg had not completely healed. That was something that would probably take a fair amount of time before it returned to normal.

Remaining at his side, Amy led him down the hallway of the little hospital that had remained left over from the town that had once occupied the area. All was going fine until Wes caught a glimpse of himself in a mirror along one of the corridors branching off the hallway. Stopping to examine himself, he now realized the extent of the damage that had been done to him in his struggle to survive and the compiled wear on his body from just a short time in the prison. The reflection staring back at him was almost unrecognizable. His head had been shaved to allow the doctor to work on the damage that had been done by the pickaxe. A number of hideous stitches ran along the side of his scalp. This sight was also accompanied by Wes's now undernourished skin and several days of stubble on his face.

"Keep moving," urged Amy as she watched a tear roll down from his now lifeless eyes. He did as she suggested, allowing her to continue escorting him down the hall.

Outside he found that Amy had brought a truck to take him down to the King's office. She had left it running, so the interior of the cab had a nice warm atmosphere. As the truck putted along the road, he looked out at his surroundings. Since the night of the attack almost two more feet of snow had fallen.

"Thank you for the ride," said Wes as Amy pulled up in front of the old high school that held the King's office inside.

"You're welcome, Wes."

Carefully lowering himself from the truck, he hobbled towards the building. This time there were no guards who interfered with his admittance, they all just stood and watched what must have looked like some hideous creature stagger through the front doors of the building they were tasked to guard. Deep down he knew this was because Amy accompanied him but that did not stop the self-conscious thoughts that his wounds brought on. That didn't matter, though, as he had no one to impress, except maybe Amy, but how long could he carry on associating with her if he was to join Abhorson's side of the battle? Amy was, in the end, just a dream and a chance to make his life feel somewhat normal.

Looking back as he went through the entrance he noticed that Amy had remained in the truck. She waved him on in encouragement as their eyes caught gazes. Returning his view forward, he continued on to his destination. Upon reaching the office door he knocked, waiting for an answer.

"Come in!" commanded the King's voice.

Wes entered. "You wanted to see me once I was up and moving."

"Yes, yes. Have a seat," directed the King while pointing at one of the chairs in front of his desk.

Doing as he was told, Wes slowly lowered his aching body into the chair.

"Mr. Petersen, are you a scotch man?"

"Not really."

"A shame, because I don't want to have a drink alone… I shall pour you a glass anyhow." The King walked over to a cabinet along the wall behind his desk and removed two glasses and a bottle from it. "This is a Dalmore 62 Single Highland Malt Scotch. Only twelve bottles were produced in 1943 and the ones that are left retail for about fifty-eight thousand dollars. So, you better damn well like it."

The King poured a little bit of the scotch into the two glasses then handed one to Wes before taking a sip out of his own. Tasting it, Wes did not care for the flavor of the drink. How could anyone justify spending that kind of money on something like this? In order to not insult the King though, he continued to work on finishing the beverage. While doing so he stared at the King, wondering how this man could send men to kill a young women and a toddler. Had he even put a thought towards such an action or had he just ordered the hit like it was as normal as swatting a fly?

The King polished off the last of the scotch in his glass and then, setting it down on the desk in front of him, he began to inform Wes as to what was to come. "I need you to be my eyes and ears in the prisoner world. I know that an attack is imminent. However, in your shape I don't feel that you are physically able to return to the mines. In most circumstances I would not care, but we have a good little arrangement going. With that said, I am putting you in charge of the library. Keep it clean and organized while you gather information on the people who mean to bring harm to me and what I have created. Also, while you are healing, I grant you the executive suite so that you may recover faster than if you were confined to some crumby apartment. How does this sound to you, Mr. Petersen?"

Leaving his hate for the man sitting in front of him buried deep inside his soul, Wes answered the King's question with as much enthusiasm as possible. "It sounds excellent to me, Sir."

"Great…now go get some rest and tomorrow I want you to work on getting me some intel on the men who are planning this revolt," stated the King as he waved at his guest, dismissing his presence from the room.

Wes left. He was caught in an onslaught of emotions as he made his way down the hall leading away from the King's office. Happiness came first as it would be nice to be in the comfort of warmth during his future time at U.C.P. After that came fear of what might happen next. This battle already had many casualties and he was sure that many more were to come. Then came anger, anger at the King, anger at Abhorson, and last but not least, anger towards himself for falling prey to their games.

Outside he found that Amy was still there, sitting in the running truck waiting for him to return. She was reading a book so she did not notice him approaching. Wes thought about what could happen to her if he did not play his cards carefully. He really did like her but Abhorson had forbidden him to see her, not to mention what the punishment would be if the King ever found out. It was a risk to her if he continued to hang around but she was the only good thing in this hell. What would he do? What could he do? It was a risk but he decided that they could continue without the King knowing for the time being. As for Abhorson, he figured that he could just tell him it was imperative to the objective that he remained close with her. He could explain that she is a source of information. As he climbed into the truck with Amy he decided he would fight to be with her because she was the only thing that reminded him that there was good in the world whether they were on the same side or not.

"Hey," said Amy as she looked up from her book, "how was your meeting with Mr. King?"

"I suppose it was as good as it could have gone under the circumstances."

"That's good." She reached into a bag on seat beside her removing two sandwiches. "Would you like one?" she asked.

"Sure, thank you." replied Wes as he took one of the sandwiches from Amy's hand. It was tuna with diced up dill pickles and it tasted wonderful. "This tastes amazing."

"Thanks, I whipped it up myself" said Amy, accepting the compliment that Wes had given her on a very simple sandwich. "Shall I drive you back to the hospital now?"

"Actually, I was wondering if you could stop at the library so I can go in and find a book to read. That way my night might not be quite so boring." stated Wes, although his real reason for wanting to go to the library was to check on the black book to see if his new found guardian angel had written out any new instructions for him.

"I can do that," informed Amy as she put the truck into gear and began to head towards the center of town.

Driving through the town square, Wes took note that Billy's body had been removed from sight, however the gallows still stood out in the open as a reminder to any others who may dare to disobey the rules that the King had set in place.

When Amy brought the truck to a stop at the entrance of the library Wes decided to inform her of the change in jobs that the King had bestowed upon him. "Did you know Mr. King has switched me from the mine to running the library?"

"I know…it was my idea. I figured you would enjoy it and he had been trying to figure out a new position for you away from the mine while you're recovering from your wounds," retorted Amy.

"Is that so?" he asked rhetorically while lowering himself out of the cab of the truck.

Amy smiled. "Don't take too long or I will have to come find you."

Going straight for the desk after entering the library, he found the book was gone. Where could it be? He and the masked person should have been the only ones who knew about it unless Amy had known about it. She was the only other person he had come across in the library but she would have said something about it, wouldn't she? Then it clicked…Abhorson. He had spies everywhere and seemed to know his every move. While he was in the hospital, Abhorson must have sent someone to collect the book to find out its contents. This could mean great danger for both him and his correspondent. He had to get the book back somehow.

Heading back to the front door, he realized he nearly forgot to grab a book. That would be a hard one to explain to Amy, so he grabbed the first one he saw before leaving. Amy took notice of his choice in reading material as he joined her in the vehicle and burst out laughing. It was titled *"How to Impress a Woman"*. For a moment he was confused about why she would burst out laughing then he looked down at the book and, reading the title for the first time, he too found it hard not to laugh.

"I, uh…" stuttered Wes.

"It's okay, I like you too, Wes. You don't need that silly book to impress me," Amy said while attempting to keep a straight face.

Wes was speechless; he did not know what to say. In the midst of the silence Amy leaned towards him, he did the same. Their lips met as the gap between them closed and he could feel the warmth of her lips on his. It was in this kiss that somewhere deep inside he knew there was something special about Amy. He knew he had to get them both out of the world they were trapped in. To him it was no longer if they escaped, it was when they escaped. Wes had found a reason for hope once again.

After the kiss there was no need for words. Both Amy and Wes felt the power it had on the other. His mind was racing the rest of the way back to the hospital. He knew he must come up with an elaborate plan to escape with her, but when and how still eluded him.

Before he peeled himself out of the cab he gave Amy a quick peck on the cheek in farewell. "Will I see you tomorrow?" he asked once he had his feet firmly planted on the ground in the snow.

"Probably," grinned Amy. He turned to leave, pushing the truck door closed as he did so, but she called out to him one final time. "Hey, you forgot your book."

Wes returned to face her through the open window where she handed him the book. "Thanks," he said with a smirk appearing across his face.

Walking through the hallway in the hospital back to his room, he found the place was deserted. One would think a medical center would have at least a few employees buzzing about but there was no staff and no patients besides Wes, of course. In his room, he found that his bed was made with fresh linens. The bed also happened to be quite comfortable, a fact that he had been too preoccupied to notice before. Although still early, he was tired and decided that he would go to sleep. Before climbing into the bed he tossed the book he had taken from the library into a drawer in the bedside table. He planned to return it the next day.

It was not long after crawling under the covers when sleep reached out to him. The time he had spent away from the hospital had taken an exhausting toll on his recovering body. If someone had not entered the room a few hours later, disturbing him, he may have slept through the night.

It was the sound of someone else's breathing that awakened him from his slumber. Each breath was heavy, that of a sick or dying man. Abhorson… Although the room was dark, he knew it was him. There was no light from the moon. On this night the clouds blocked it from watching over the horrors of the prison. "I know it's you," stated Wes in not much more than a murmur.

"How did your visit with Mr. King go?" asked the old man's voice.

"Good, he knows of the resistance though."

"Is that so…" Abhorson sat quiet, contemplating the news Wes had provided him. "I suppose we should give him a name, one that will make him feel like he is gaining ground towards ending the movement." said Abhorson after another pause of contemplation. "Tomorrow I shall have Viktor deliver you a piece of paper with a name on it. You must tell the King that this person is part of the resistance. Can you handle that?"

"Yes," replied Wes.

"Good. Now, do you have anything else to tell me?"

"Well, I had an idea…"

"Go on," urged Abhorson.

"That woman guard, Amy. I think it would be beneficial if I continue to befriend her as she is very high ranking and may allow me to get closer to the King." Wes had joined the game. He was no longer just a pawn, he was now a player. If Abhorson could manipulate him, then why could he not do the same in return?

"Smart, I guess you are more intelligent than I thought," acknowledged Abhorson as Wes listened to his cane tapping its way towards the door.

"More than you know," he mumbled under his breath as Abhorson's presence vanished into the hall leaving him alone in the dark, pondering over what his next move would be.

Chapter 9

As dawn broke with the light from the horizon filling the room, Wes awoke. The majority of the night since Abhorson's departure had been spent plotting what was to come next. He never did figure out a definite plan so he would simply allow the next turn in the game to be made by one of the other players. His plan was to remain, in their eyes, as just a piece to be moved while he slowly worked his own angle to victory.

It was not long after daybreak that Dr. Cho arrived to check in on him.

"Good morning, Mr. Petersen." he said cheerfully as he went about checking his vitals. "Everything looks good. I don't need you to spend any more nights here although I would like you to stop by in a couple days so I can check on the progress of your healing and make sure no infections develop."

Wes nodded to the Doctor in agreement. After Dr. Cho left the room he decided to walk down to dining hall for something to eat, he was famished from the lack of food in his system from the previous days.

When he entered the hall all the men looked in his direction. He noticed the hatred towards him that had earlier been in their eyes had been replaced with respect. He could only assume they all believed that he had single handily taken down the killer in the mine. Even though the views people had of him may have changed, nobody dared to join him at his table and he ate alone once again.

After breakfast he decided to make his way over to the library. He had the book he had taken stuffed in his coat so that he could return it. About halfway through his journey Viktor stepped out from behind a building that he was passing. Without a word the man handed over a crumpled piece of paper before he turned and bolted down an ally. Opening the paper, Wes found a single name written across it, "Michael Hornley." It was a name he did not recognize. This was probably for the better as he had a hunch that poor Michael would be falling victim to some horrible act in the very near future. Yes, he knew that when he turned over the name to the King it would result in someone's death, but he no longer cared. The only people who needed to survive, in his mind, were he and Amy. Besides, he was not the one doing the killing. This man would simply be a casualty of war between the King and Abhorson.

He considered going directly to the King with the name he was handed, then thought better of it. If he went right away the King would know that something was up, he had only just assigned him to the task the day before. He also had to develop a plausible story as to how he knew this Michael guy was part of the revolt against the King. With that thought, he continued towards the library where he decided he would wait until mid-afternoon before paying a visit to the King.

The library was void of humans, as it usually seemed to be. He returned the book he had gotten the day before to the shelves then he decided to check on the black book again. It was still gone but where it had been now held a note that read, "I am sorry, I had to destroy the book for fear that my identity would be discovered. You are constantly being followed and it is not just I who is doing so. I will continue to watch out for you. Please make sure to destroy this letter when you are done reading it." The words on the paper relieved him of a fear that the book had come into the hands of one of his enemies.

He worked away in the library all morning sorting and organizing the shelves that lined the room. Just when he was beginning to get hungry for lunch Amy showed up to surprise him.

"Wes!" she called as she entered the building.

"One sec," he replied from the back of the room as he made his way up to the front to greet his visitor.

"I brought you some lunch," she said as she removed a thermos and a pair of mugs from her bag. "It is homemade soup, a clam chowder recipe that my mother taught me when I was a little girl."

"Wonderful, I was just starting to get hungry," he exclaimed as he led her to the back table where they could sit and eat.

After pouring some soup into a mug for Wes she poured some for herself. "I see that you have made some progress in here already."

"A little."

"I hope it is better than working at the mine."

"Oh yes, of course," he said as he took a sip from his mug. "I am sorry that I am not much company today. I have a lot on my mind."

"That's fine, I best be going soon anyways. I will leave the thermos here with you so you can have more of the soup if you would like. Just take it up to the house with you tonight and I will stop by and pick it up."

"Sure," he said, giving her a slight smile as she got up to leave.

When she was gone he decided he had waited long enough. He would now take the name Viktor had given him to the King. Slowly he made his way over to the old high school to find the man he was pretending to work for. He was able to find him in his office as usual.

"Come in," called the King when Wes knocked.

"I have a name for you."

"You work fast. How were you able to come across this information in such a short period of time?"

"They have a suspicion that we are working together. I was approached by a man and he attempted to recruit me to their side, suggested that I spy on you for them. Become a double agent of sorts, I guess," Wes lied, hoping that the King would be unable to see through his charade."

"What was your response to this proposition?" questioned the King.

"I told him I would think about it, of course."

"Good, this may be the opportunity we need to gain insight into the plans that these infidels are making… Now, what is the name of the man that approached you?"

"Michael Hornley"

"Okay, I will deal with this Hornley fellow. If anyone comes to you again, agree to working with them. I could use a man on the inside.

"Will do."

"Of course you will," said the King as a grin emerged on his face. "Now go…and maybe take the rest of the afternoon off since you have done such a wonderful job thus far."

Wes nodded as he left the room. Deep down it hurt knowing that he had just condemned a man to death. Lacking anything better to do he decided to walk up to the house for a soak in the tub. His body ached and the pain only increased from the distance he had to travel to make it there. It was all worthwhile, though, when he slowly let his body slide into the depths of the tub's water.

It was when he had finished in the washroom and began to dress that there was a knock on the door. It was still early in the afternoon, who could it be? Opening it he found a guard waiting.

"Can I help you?" he asked, curious as to why he was in the presence of one of the guards.

"Mr. King is requesting an audience of all personnel and prisoners in the town square in one hour."

Wes immediately knew what this was. Everyone was being summoned to watch another execution. "Thank you for letting me know," he said, acknowledging the information that had been relayed to him before closing the door in the guard's face. This was not something he wanted to watch but he knew that if he did not go he could be the next to be sentenced to death.

The walk to the center of town would take up the majority of the time he had before everyone was due to arrive so he quickly finished off the rest of the soup Amy had left him before heading to the King's show.

When he arrived a large crowd had already gathered. The gallows had been removed, a new contraption replacing it. The King's men had made short work of that. In the center of the square now sat a giant caldron with a metal cross that rose up into the air from its center. Underneath the caldron a fire burned, boiling its contents. Everyone stared at the man tied to the cross. His arms were stretched out across the horizontal bar. This was a scene taken from the bible, only modified slightly to serve better purpose. The man who had been stripped naked was positioned high enough from the boiling water so the cold would slowly blacken his skin with frost bite, yet he was low enough that the steam from below would keep him from freezing to death.

This was no execution, this was pure torture. It was set up to disturb anyone who bore witness. Death would be a sweet release compared to this evil. He could see that the man was coming to from an unconscious state. It would only be a moment before chaos would break loose.

Upon awakening, the man began to scream as the winter air nipped at every surface of his body. The temperature was easily below minus thirty Celsius. Someone in the crowd shouted in anger before charging towards the torture instrument to cut the man down. As this brave onlooker reached a place where he would be able to aid the poor man, a gunshot resounded through the crisp air and he dropped to the ground screaming in pain while still in midstride. This sent murmurs throughout the crowd. Everyone looked around to see if they could spot the shooter but no one was able to.

After the incident everyone slowly backed away from the horror and no one dared to offer any assistance to the man on the ground who was now choking on his own blood or the individual strapped to the pole awaiting his slow, agonizing death. It was out of fear for their own lives that they left the two gentlemen to die.

Wes remained watching out of amazement of the inhumanity that unveiled itself before him. Most of the crowd left, leaving only him and a few other inmates listening to the screams of the dying. Finally, fifteen minutes after the gun shot had rung out, a guard carrying a pistol in his hand walked up to the man who was slowly bleeding out from his wound. It was the sound of the second shot that raised Wes out of the trance he was caught in.

Following that final shot that put the prisoner out of his misery, screams still filled the air from the other inmate who remained caught on the edge of freezing to death. The guard paid no attention to him though. His eyes had shifted towards Wes. The guard then raised his gun and pointed it directly at him. Terror gripped his very soul as he stared at the gun that was focused on him.

"Mr. Petersen," called the individual with the gun, "Mr. King would like to have a word with you immediately. I suggest that you come with me."

Wes followed the order and the man lowered the gun as he did what was directed. The entire trip to see the King, who still remained in his office, was driven by the guard who refused to holster his weapon, although it was a relief that he did not feel it necessary to keep the barrel aimed in his direction.

At the front entrance the guard finally allowed Wes to continue on his own through the building. He burst through the office door without knocking. The King was seated at his desk, startled by the sudden intrusion.

"What the hell, boy? You're supposed to knock."

The King's comment only fueled his rage. "Why was I brought here at gun point? I thought we were on the same side," he yelled, completely ignoring the King's question.

"I don't know anything about the gunpoint stuff, although I did send one of my men to fetch you. I have a proposition for you," informed the King.

"What is it?" he asked with a more calming tone.

"I have been thinking and I would like you to become one of my guards. I feel that it will give more incentive for my enemies to try and recruit you to their ranks. Of course this will be to our advantage... What do you say?"

He thought for a moment and decided it would be a perfect opportunity to gain some more leverage for himself. "Sounds like a good idea."

"Of course it's a good idea. I will have Miss Kale pick you up at seven tomorrow morning to begin your training."

"Thank you for the opportunity, Sir," he said with gratitude. He was excited that he would get to spend the day with Amy.

While he was leaving the office, the King called after him. "Don't disappoint me, Mr. Petersen."

He was almost skipping with joy on his walk back to the house. The fact that some poor soul was being tortured to death just down the road because of him had fled his mind.

Chapter 10

The following morning Wes woke early and was ready long before Amy was due to pick him up for the start of his training. He wondered what it would consist of, possibly some firearms instruction or maybe techniques to apprehend the prisoners. It didn't matter though, he was just happy that he would be able to spend the day with the closest person he had to being a friend without having to remain hidden from the prying eyes of his enemies.

When he heard the knock on the front door, Wes rushed over to it to greet his instructor.

"Are you ready?" asked Amy upon his hello.

"I am."

"Great, let's go. We have a long day ahead of us," she said, leading him out to the waiting truck.

The venture in the truck took him further from the town's limits than he had gone before. It was nearly forty minutes cruising at a hasty pace before they rounded a bend revealing a building that resembled an old warehouse.

"What is this place?" asked Wes as the truck approached the front of the structure that stood erect before them.

"This is our storage facility. I have set up some training equipment here so that we are not stuck out in the cold while working on your skills," answered Amy as she pushed a button on a remote that sent out a signal causing a big door on the warehouse to open, thus allowing her to pull the truck right into the interior of the building.

Wes was amazed at the capacity of the first room they entered. It was filled with vehicles. There were several trucks and buses, along with a dozen brand new snowmobiles. As surprising as all that was there was one vehicle that his eyes were particularly drawn to.

In the far back corner of the room sat a 1947 Cadillac convertible that appeared to be all original. Wes was drawn to it, he was almost drooling over the beauty the car had compared to its modern day successors.

"Don't touch that!" called Amy from behind him as he was making his way over to the work of art that sat parked before him. "It is Mr. King's prized possession."

"Okay, I understand," he replied as he returned to his companion's side.

Leading him into the next room, Amy flipped a switch that illuminated the mass of area, one light flickering on at a time as the power raced through the connecting wires. This room was of much more interest to Wes, it looked like it was set up for military training. One wall was lined with a variety of weapons from pistols to shotguns, with a few assault rifles mixed into the bunch. At the far side of the room a shooting range had been constructed. There were also various other training apparatuses set up, such as an obstacle course and weight lifting area.

"Wow, this is quite the place!" exclaimed Wes. "Is there any more to it?"

"Yes, one more room. That is where the uranium gets stored."

"Ah... So, where do we start?" he asked, rubbing his hands together in a gesture of anticipation for the day's activities.

"Well, how is your shooting ability?"

"I have never shot a gun before in my life."

"Then I guess we start there." Amy moved towards the wall of guns, retrieving what Wes could only assume was a nine millimeter. Handing it over to him, she then proceeded to lead him over to the shooting range.

"Now what?"

"You shoot the target," she replied sarcastically, followed by a slight giggle.

"Oh, you're funny," replied Wes with a slight laugh. He then raised the gun, pointing it in the direction of one of the targets on the range. He attempted to pull the trigger but it would not budge under the pressure of his finger. "What the hell?" he rhetorically asked himself.

Amy was standing, watching him play with the gun in an attempt to figure it out. After a few moments of allowing him to grow frustrated she finally piped up. "You have a couple of issues, Wes."

"A couple?" he groaned. He was sure he was making a complete fool of himself. "How do I make this thing work?"

"First, I would suggest putting some ammunition into the gun."

"That may be a good idea," he said, trying to shrug off the embarrassment of not thinking about having bullets in the gun. "Where can I get some ammo for it?"

"Right here," replied Amy. She walked over to him then began to show him how to load the gun safely with the bullets she removed from her jacket pocket.

"Thanks."

"No problem," she said with a smirk.

Wes once again took aim and Amy stepped back. The second attempt at pulling the trigger resulted just as it had first time around. This time he was able to hide his frustration and he looked back at his trainer for a sign of help.

"The safety is on," she grinned, trying to hold back a laugh.

"Duh!" mumbled Wes under his breath to himself. The third try was the charm. When he pulled the trigger the gun fired. Then he fired a second and third time at the target. His ears rang as the sound of the shots echoed throughout the room.

"Put the safety back on!" yelled Amy, her voice reaching him over the ringing in his ears.

Wes did as he was told then stood and waited while Amy retrieved the target he had shot at. "How did I do?" he asked in curiosity as she returned to where he was standing.

With a laugh she said, "You missed every shot."

Wes felt defeated but, even though he had not hit his mark with a single shot, he knew it was not his fault since he had never handled a gun before. "Well, they say practice makes perfect. I guess I just need a little more practice."

"You just need to know how to shoot a gun first. After that your accuracy will come. Let me show you." Amy took a step forward, planted her feet, straightened her posture and then took three shots. The target she picked for herself to aim at was even further back than the one he had chosen. When she was done she gently placed the gun on a table that was set up a few feet away from where they were standing before going to retrieve her target. Upon her return she showed it to him. All three holes where the bullets had hit were clustered in the center of the bull's eye.

"Well, you're way better than me," Wes said with a smile.

"With practice, you will be just as good. Just make sure your posture is good, take a deep breath before you fire and squeeze the trigger, don't pull it. Can you handle that?"

"I think so."

"Great, now try again," she insisted.

Wes picked up the gun, doing exactly as he had just been instructed to do. He hit the target two out of three shots. They were far from bull's eyes but it was an improvement.

"Good job."

"Thanks, your advice helped."

"Why don't you practice a little more then we will go for lunch," suggested Amy.

"Sounds like a plan. Do I get to use big guns after lunch?" he asked, winking at her.

"Not a chance!" she replied, giggling at his not-so-funny joke.

Over the following hour, Wes went through about forty-five rounds with the pistol he was learning to shoot with. By the end of the session he was consistently able to hit the target every time he fired but the bullets weren't hitting the target quite where he was aiming for. He had completely lost track of time when Amy informed him that it was time to go for lunch. He nodded in agreement before unloading what was left in the clip and returning the gun to its home on the wall.

"I was thinking we could go out to the cabin for lunch. I took some food out there this morning and lit a fire to warm the place up."

"Great," he replied and his mind went back to the last time they were at the cabin and how beautiful a place it was.

"The truck won't be able to get there so we will take snowmobiles. I got them ready while you were working on your shooting skills,"

Amy said as she led him outside to the two running machines that awaited them.

"I get my own?" he asked in surprise.

"I don't see why not, although I would not mention it to Mr. King. He might not like it that much."

"Oh, I will be sure not to say anything," he told her, a bit of fear simmering deep inside, for if the King found out it could be disastrous.

Amy jumped onto the first of the two sleds and took off so he climbed onto the second. He had only ridden a snowmobile once before on his own, that was a few years ago when he had gone on a trip to the mountains with some friends. It came back to him very fast as he raced to keep up with Amy who had tamed her sled to the point where it was an extension of her body. He knew she was not riding to her full potential, if she did then he would be left behind in a cloud of snow. She kept herself just far enough ahead that he was forced to push the limits of his own riding capability in order to keep up. Even if he did lose sight of her, which he did at a couple points along the way, he would be able to follow the tracks that her sled left in its wake.

The ride was fun. It was like a game of tag only Wes was bad at the game so he always remained "it". Finally Amy slowed down as the two of them approached the little cabin. The view on this day was just as beautiful, if not more magnificent, than he remembered it from before.

Shutting off the machines, they entered the cabin together. The fire that had been lit earlier in the day had been reduced to not much more than a few hot coals but its heat still remained in the atmosphere of the one room building. There was wood stacked beside the stone fireplace, some cut up as kindling. Wes went to work attempting to rouse the fire back to life. As he worked at his task, Amy set up lunch on an old wood table that was positioned by the front window, giving whoever was seated at it a glimpse of the cabin's glorious view.

Soon the fire was once again roaring; its heat radiating throughout the entire square footage of the room. The two of them joined together at the table where they began to start on their lunch. Amy had prepared a feast consisting of soup, sandwiches, cut up vegetables and a banana loaf for dessert.

The flames cast shadows on the walls as they danced to the crackling of the fire. The essence of the theatrics the flames produced was peaceful entertainment, enjoyed by its audience throughout the meal. After Wes and Amy finished eating she packed away the leftovers while he stoked the fire for its second act.

As the fire danced on, the two current inhabitants of the cabin sat on a couch positioned in front of the fire's stage. Wes wrapped his arm around Amy as they chatted about their dreams in life, both of them knowing that their dreams would only come true if they were able to escape the hold that Uranium City Prison had on them.

It was not long before they fell asleep, Amy remaining in his embrace. The day slipped away as they slept in the comfort of the warmth that radiated from the fireplace and it was dark when Wes finally awoke. He gave Amy a gentle shake to rouse her.

"What?" she asked in a whisper without opening her eyes.

"We fell asleep. It is now dark out and we should probably head back," he explained to her as she sat up, stretching her arms.

"Oh, you're right. We better get going," she replied as she rushed over to the hook she had hung her coat on. She pulled it over her shoulders, going out the door to start the snowmobiles as she did so, in an attempt to give them time to warm up from the cold before being put to use.

Wes casually stood up looking at the fireplace; the logs that he had placed in the flames earlier were now nothing but a few hot coals. He then procured his own jacket from where it hung, putting it on and joining Amy outside.

The sleds were running and she was staring up into the night sky. He assumed she was gazing upon the stars or possibly the northern lights. Following her line of sight, his eyes caught hold of what had captured her attention. A small plane was flying overhead, losing altitude at a rapid pace.

"There aren't supposed to be any planes up here," choked Amy, her statement directed towards herself in an attempt to make some sense out of what was happening.

Wes starred in astonishment as the plane vanished into the tree tops a few kilometers away. "We must go and help!" he exclaimed as he watched her just stand and stare at the spot that she had lost sight of the plane.

Smoke was rising up from the crash site. It felt like forever before she spoke. "Yes, let's go."

Wes and Amy left in a hurry, heading towards the ever growing tower of smoke. The engines of the snowmobiles roared as they were pushed to their limits in an effort to arrive at the plane's wreckage in a timely manner. He nearly crashed twice, barely missing trees that seemed to pop up out of thin air directly in front of his speeding machine.

The plane had gone down in a small clearing; shrapnel was spread across the area. Flames were beginning to grow from the aircraft's carcass. Wes and Amy brought their vehicles to a stop a short distance from the wreckage. The sight was surreal. It was unlikely anyone would have been able to survive such a traumatic accident.

"I don't think anyone could have pulled through that." spoke Amy in a deep tone of sympathy.

Wes began to nod in agreement when he caught a movement from inside the crumpled heap of metal. "Look!" he yelled as he jumped off his sled, racing towards the flames that were still increasing in volume.

"Careful!" she called after him but he paid no attention to her word of warning as he continued to rush to the aid of what he thought may be a survivor.

As he approached, someone was climbing out of the fire that had now nearly engulfed the entire plane. His eyes met with the distant gaze of the man who was now stumbling from the disaster. When the man had escaped the wrath of the flames, he collapsed face down into the snow. Wes knew he had to get the victim further away from the plane in case the fuel tank decided to explode, which would send both him and the collapsed survivor to a fiery death.

Grabbing the man, he turned him face up. It was at that moment that he recognized this particular individual. The man lying in the snow before him was none other than Scott Loken, his roommate, the man responsible for his imprisonment in this Hell. Ignoring the urge to leave Scott for dead, he pulled the unconscious body to safety. "What was Scott doing here?" he wondered out loud, but in a low enough tone that Amy couldn't make out what he said.

"What?" she asked as she came over from her sled to help.

"Nothing" he replied, deciding that for the moment it would be safer for all three of them if his and Scott's previous relationship was not known. "I was just talking to myself."

"Oh. I was just thinking it would be best if you left and headed back to the house for the night. Mr. King or one of the other guards will have noticed the plane and will be sending out a search party and there is no explanation as to why we were out here together at such a late hour. I don't want either of us to get into trouble." she explained.

"What about him?" he asked, indicating Scott.

"I'll get him to the hospital" she assured him.

After a moment of hesitation Wes decided she was right, it would be better if he was not around when the others arrived to investigate the crash. "Will you let me know how things go?"

"Of course I will, now get going. Just park your sled behind the house so that no one sees it. I will come by in the morning to collect it and get it back before anyone realizes it is missing."

With a nod he left her to tend to Scott's unmoving body. The roar of other snowmobiles was fast approaching as he left on his. He made sure to go a different way so that he did not meet any of the other guards along the path who were traveling towards him.

Once he arrived back at the so called executive suite, he stashed the snow mobile behind the house. He knew he should go to bed and attempt to get some sleep, but with the nap at the cabin and Scott's face plastered in his mind, all he could do was lie in bed and pray for the sweet release from reality that sleep offered.

Chapter 11

Wes awoke exhausted. It was still dark outside but the bedroom window allowed for a bit of the moon's lights to enter the premises. Most of the night's hours thus far had been spent tossing and turning, fighting for sleep to come. So many new questions were added to his already large list of unanswered ones. A knock on the door had roused him. Fumbling through the dark areas of the house that the moon failed to reach, he made his way over to the front door. To his surprise, it was Amy. She looked as if she had not yet been to bed.

"Amy, what are you doing here?"

"I wanted to update you on the situation."

"Yes?"

"There were two men onboard the plane. The pilot died instantly, the other man is alive but unconscious in our hospital, the same room that you were treated in."

"You look beat."

"I am. I haven't gone to bed yet."

"What time is it?"

Amy glanced at her watch. "Just after four AM."

"You can sleep in my bed if you would like. I am up now and don't think I could sleep anymore."

"No I better go home," she tried to explain as she fought to keep her eyes open from exhaustion. "On second thought, I will take you up on your offer. Just don't let me sleep for too long."

Wes led her to the bedroom where she collapsed on the bed. It only took a few seconds before she passed out. He slowly slipped out of the room, closing the door behind him cautiously so to not wake her. He wanted to pay a visit to the hospital room that now housed his old roommate.

Considering using the sled for his trip over to visit Scott, he ended up deciding against it. The noise from the engine would draw attention and attention was something that would get a person in trouble in this place.

Staying in the shadows, he made his way towards the hospital. There were few people out at this time. Everyone was either sleeping or working a night shift in one of the mines. The few souls who were scattered about were mostly guards on night patrol. Wes made sure to avoid the town center for the nightmares that had taken place there were too recent in his memory to dare come in contact with again. From a distance he could see the light cast by the fire that still burned, boiling the contents of the cauldron that kept the prisoner who was suspended above it caught somewhere between life and death.

The lights at the hospital were all turned off for the night. It gave the place an eerie feeling. Wes found the main entrance unlocked; no wonder it had been so easy for people to drop by during the night when he had been cooped up there. Now the role was reversed and he was the one sneaking in to consult with a patient. There was a good chance that Scott would be drugged up and asleep. This trip was more to confirm that his eyes had not played some sort of trick on him and to make sure that the man inside was really Scott Loken.

There was a faint light trickling in from the hall windows that allowed him to move through the corridors of the hospital with ease. As he passed the same mirror that had captured his attention a few days before, he noticed he was already starting to look healthier. He no longer looked like some zombie that had crawled up from a deep dark grave.

The door to Scott's room was left ajar. He pushed it open slowly as he slipped inside. Scott was lying in the bed, an IV running to his arm. Wes presumed it was some sort of pain killer, possibly morphine. Taking a close look at the limp form under the covers, he confirmed that it was indeed Scott. His former roommate looked as if he had gone to hell and back but that was not true. There was no going back. Scott had now joined him in hell, for what reason? That was unknown. Something seemed off. If Scott had been involved in the plan to get him sent to this place, then what was he doing here?

With the confirmation that it was indeed Scott who had been aboard the downed plane, he decided that he would make his way back to the house to check up on Amy. As he was exiting the room however, he heard talking from down the hall. Three voices were apparent. He was not the only one who had decided to pay a visit to Scott Loken under the shadows of the night.

Without further hesitation he ducked back into Scott's room. There was a closet across from the bed that he could take refuge in and he quickly dashed over to it, hiding inside. Just as he was able to get the door sealed, the men from down the hall entered. He was able to peek through the slats of the closet door, giving him a view of Scott's company.

He had presumed that there were three individuals due to the number of voices he had heard but there was actually four. The fourth man remained quiet while the others continued to speak. Wes recognized all of the men except for the silent man. Dr. Cho, Abhorson and Jack were the ones he was able to recognize. It occurred to him that the fourth man was most likely just a piece of muscle. He looked young and strong.

Remaining still, he silently listened to the conversation that was taking place just a few feet away from him.

"How long before he wakes up?" Abhorson asked, directing the question to the doctor.

"I have him on a sedative, if I did not he would already have come to."

"Very good, Dr. Cho, you are proving to be very valuable. However, we cannot let Mr. Petersen find out about Mr. Loken's arrival. Mr. Petersen has gained a powerful position in this game. If he were to find out what Loken knows, it could spell disaster for our plan."

The room was silent for a moment, and then Jack spoke. "What do we need Wes for anyways? We know when and how we are going to strike. He is just a liability. We could just kill him and be done with the problem."

"That may be so but at the moment Mr. Petersen is on our side. I have also planted the idea in his head to kill the King. Until Wes is a definite threat, we must continue to use him as one of our pawns," explained Abhorson.

"I can keep him under for as long as you need, Abhorson," offered Dr. Cho.

"No, no, let him wake up. The King will take care of him. No one is allowed to arrive in this place uninvited. I suppose that Mr. Loken will be lucky to make the end of the week once the King has a hold of him."

"When do we make the attack?" asked the doctor.

"Soon, the King is planning on hosting a large party at his mansion for all the officials that support this prison. Many of the guards will be up there guarding the place, leaving Uranium City for the taking. Once we have control, we will move towards the mansion and take out the King himself, providing Mr. Petersen does not do the job for us before then."

Jack began to speak in not much more than a whisper. In order to hear what was being said by the man, Wes pressed his ear against the door in an attempt at making out the faint words. It was at that point that he knocked over a broom that was leaning up in the closet, causing a slight thud when it hit the floor.

"What was that?" asked Abhorson, as all four of the men's gazes turned in the direction of Wes's hiding place. "Go check it out, Fritz."

The man who had remained silent through the entire conversation, now known too Wes as Fritz, began to move towards the closet. He was petrified and he had no escape route.

Frozen, he tried to plan a way out of the predicament he was now faced with. If he were to be caught, based on the conversation he had overheard, it would probably mean death. Fritz began to open the door. Wes's only option was to make a run for it. He was sure that Abhorson and Jack had no chance of catching him and Dr. Cho didn't look all that physically fit. The only real obstacle was Fritz.

As soon as the door had been opened by the silent man, he slammed himself into the unsuspecting henchman. The plan almost failed to work but, with a bit of a teeter Fritz lost his balance, falling to the floor. Wes didn't stop. He just kept running right past the three others who stood in shock from the surprise of his grand escape.

The shock only lasted a second. It was only a few steps out the door before he heard Abhorson yell "Get him!" Glancing back, he could see that Fritz was up and moving again. He came out of the hospital room door barrelling down the hall towards him like a bull on steroids. Pushing on, Wes ran right out the front doors of the hospital, headed to an area that was more densely filled with buildings, hoping that he would be able to lose the predator that was on his heels.

"Get back here you fool!" yelled Fritz, revealing a heavy German accent.

Wes did not even look back when the man chasing him yelled. He now arrived on one of the main streets. Fritz had lost sight of him. This was his chance to escape. The library stood to his right and he quickly rushed inside before Fritz could round the corner and spot him. The lights were out, which was optimal for seeking shelter from the sights of his enemies. Keeping an eye on the glass front door he watched as the German passed on by.

For a moment he thought he was safe. Unfortunately, the feeling didn't even have time to settle before Viktor came crashing through the library door. He had a bat of some sort in his hand. Before Wes could even stand from his crouched position, Viktor swung the bat knocking him unconscious with a single blow.

When he came to he had no idea of how long he had been out for but it had been enough time for his captors to tie him to a chair. Five men now stood in front of him. They had been in conversation but had stopped in the midst of it, focusing their attention on their prisoner as he awoke. The five men were the four from the hospital, the addition was Viktor. He knew this was not going to end well. He had become a liability to Abhorson's plan and, as a result, the need for his elimination had arisen.

"I am so pleased that you could join us" Abhorson said, stepping forward. "I am, however, not a fan of eavesdroppers. " Wes attempted to provide an argument but Abhorson cut off his attempt before a full word had even made it out of his mouth. "I suppose you now know I will have to kill you, which is a real shame. You showed potential."

Wes, in his head, was praying for a miracle that would allow for an escape. Where was his guardian angel in the mask now? Had the masked person been a follower of Abhorson all along, and was now obsolete due to Abhorson's desire to end his life? "Why must you kill me? I can still be of value and I wish to kill the King with my own hands" he stated, lying. Yes, he did want the King dead but he was not capable of taking the man's life. He hoped this little ploy would at the very least buy him some time, if not save him, by convincing Abhorson of his usefulness.

"Oh, shut up you fool. I know you have been trying to play me. You are in love with that female guard. I am at least letting you die without you knowing the real truth about who she is. No matter who won this battle, you were never going to leave this hell. This is the end for you, Mr. Petersen" Abhorson stated in a calm cool tone.

He was confused, what did this monster mean about not knowing who Amy really was? The complications were already clear, no matter how far up the ranks he climbed he would always be a prisoner and Amy would always be a guard in the King's eyes. Wes's train of thought was then interrupted by a command from Abhorson. He was instructing Viktor and Fritz to burn down the library with him still inside, strapped to the chair. Without a word of protest the two men nodded in acceptance of the order they had been burdened with.

Abhorson, Jack and Dr. Cho departed, leaving Fritz and Viktor to complete their task.

"Nice easy job" said Viktor to Fritz, as he began to pile a bunch of books to start the fire with.

"Yes, this place should burn well with all these books. It is a shame though, as I don't believe in burning the words of all these great authors," replied Fritz

Wes remained silent. His eyes darted around the room, feeding his brain with the visuals needed to develop a plan on how to remove himself from the mess he was trapped in. Nothing came to mind, though. He was, as they say, screwed.

Once the preparations were complete for creating an ideal environment for the fire to grow, Viktor removed a brass lighter from the breast pocket of his coat. Lighting it, he tossed it onto the pile of books that had just been created.

The flames quickly began to grow, engulfing the pile of literature. Fritz and Viktor fled once the flames had grown to an acceptable size and they were sure that the fire would take, destroying the library along with everything within. Once again Wes was faced with the fear of death, just as he had on a regular basis since his arrival in Uranium City. Only this time, he did not even possess a chance to fight for survival. There was no hope.

The room temperature began to rise in a matter of moments along with the choking strength of the smoke that was starting to prey on Wes's lungs. Watching was all he could do as the embrace of the fire's elements began to chip away at his ability to sustain life.

Making peace with his death, he closed his eyes in order to picture Amy one last time. It was a shame that he had only had such a short period of time to get to know the woman he knew he could love for the rest of his life. It was in this period of thought that a bus came crashing through the rear wall of the library, traveling in reverse. The sudden impact left a gaping hole next to where he was positioned in his execution chair. The bus was one of the ones that were used to transport prisoners. Climbing out through the front door was his guardian angel, the individual who still bore a mask to hide the identity of who had been helping him in his times of need.

He was losing the ability to focus as he continued to inhale the smoke. His last vision was that of the masked person grabbing hold of the chair and dragging it and him out as a single unit through the large opening in the wall.

The fresh, cool, winter air grazing his skin slowly brought him back to reality. He was alive, once again due to whoever hid behind the mask. At some point between being dragged out of the fire and returning to reality, the chair he was tied to had been broken in order to free its prisoner. The remains of it lay a few feet from the burnt out rubble that lay smouldering where the library once stood. People were standing all around the remains of the building. He had been dragged a great distance away and no one seemed to notice him. Everyone's attention was on the bus that sat amidst the destruction, all presumably wondering how it got there.

It was bright outside as he slipped away from the scene. A good part of the day had passed since he had left the house in the middle of the night. He just wanted to return to the little home he was granted as part of his deal with the King. A warm bath would do wonders on his aching, soot covered body. He also had a desire to check and see if Amy still remained asleep in his bed. She had been beyond tired and may have slept through the events of the day, although he did have a hard time believing that she would not have been radioed in to provide some kind of help in the clean up or extinguishing of the fire.

Amy was gone when he returned to the house. He was slightly relieved. It would be better if she did not see him in the condition he was in. Heading straight for the tub he drew himself a hot bath. The water was pure ecstasy as he slid into its depths. Time slowly slipped away as he scrubbed the silt from his skin. When the water had cooled he climbed out, reaching for a towel to dry off with.

Feeling refreshed, he checked the fridge to see if Amy had left behind any of her wonderful cooking. Sadly that was not the case, so he decided to head down to the dining hall to fetch some grub.

Now that he was clean and all evidence of his entanglement with the fire was washed away, he had no issues walking through the small crowd that still remained at the site of where the library once stood. All that was left was a small tower of smoke that was slowly petering off.

Searching the faces of the crowd, he was unable to find Amy's. She must have been somewhere else. Once he was sure she was not there he continued on his route to the dining hall. It was too early for the dinner rush; therefore it was lacking a large number of patrons. Inside he was served a simple grilled cheese sandwich. The lady at the food counter had said that all the commotion regarding the fire resulted in a proper meal not being prepared so it would be simple meals for all the prisoners on this evening.

Wes was worried that Abhorson or one of his minions would come into the hall and spot him however he did not believe they would attempt to harm him out in the open. Considering this idea, he realized that providing they had not noticed the burnt out bus, they probably still assumed he was dead which was a good possibility because the chances were that they wanted to get as far as possible away from the crime so they could not be tied to the act.

Once he was finished with his very meager meal, he decided to head back to the house. He wanted to go to sleep early so that he could get up in the middle of the night and pay Scott another visit, hopefully this time without running into Abhorson.

On the way back to the house, he noticed that the King had come to view the devastation that the fire had caused earlier in the day. Not wanting to get caught up, he changed the route that he had been planning on taking by ducking down an alleyway before the King had a chance to notice him. His attempt at dodging the King proved to be successful and the detour only cost him a couple minutes which for sure would have been longer if he had been forced to converse with the King.

The door to the house was slightly open when he arrived. This was odd, as he was sure that he had closed the door completely when he had left. He began to grow worried. Someone could be lurking inside waiting to kill him so he prepared himself for a struggle as he pushed the door open the rest of the way. Sitting in a chair at the kitchen table was Amy. She had her head down on the table. He was relieved that the intruder was a friend and not an enemy. Wes made a mental note that always being afraid was something that would not work for him. The following day he planned to go to the King and give up Abhorson's name.

"Amy?" asked Wes, with a tone of concern in his voice.

"Yes?" she replied as she raised her head and turned to face him. She had a burn mark on her left cheek.

"Oh my god, are you ok?" he said, rushing across the room for closer inspection of her wound. As he got closer he noticed that she also had a bad burn on her right arm.

"I am fine. It's just a little burn." She turned her face slightly, keeping the burn away from his view. "I woke up to my radio buzzing away in regards to the fire. When you weren't here I thought maybe you were at the library. I rushed down there and you were nowhere to be seen so I thought maybe you were still inside. I got burned in my attempt to rush in through the front door to get you and head to back out. I thought you were dead, Wes!" A few tears began to roll down her face.

"Hey, it's okay. I'm okay," he said in as comforting a tone as possible. He knew deep down that at the moment he may not actually be okay at all. He had no idea how many people would be hunting him once word got out that he was still alive.

"I realized something though..." Amy looked into his eyes, "I am falling in love with you."

"And I, you," he replied as he wrapped his arms around her in an attempt to provide comfort.

She proceeded to kiss him, and he her. Then stepping away from his embrace, she took his hand and led him to the bedroom. Stepping through the door, he closed it behind them. The outside world became non-existent in their minds as the door shut with a slight thud. Their actions did not escalate; they simply lay on the bed holding each other in comfort as they drifted into a deep sleep.

Chapter 12

Wes awoke. Amy was still fast asleep at his side. For a moment he felt happy, until he remembered where he was. The day ahead of him proved to be challenging. The game he was playing had moved into what he believed was going to be the final act. It was no longer a battle in which he could play both sides. It was now a war and in war one must do things that ordinarily would not be done. He had to side with one of his enemies in order to defeat the greater foe. In this case, he was siding with the King. The other thing that was on his agenda for the day was to look into Scott's appearance at the prison as it was still a mystery as to why he showed up, or at least it was a mystery to him.

Glancing towards the clock he realized that it was still very early. He could sneak out and go over to the hospital before everyone else in the prison was up and moving for the day. The only complication was to do it without disturbing Amy. Sliding his arm out from under her, he slowly crept from the room. Ideally he would be back before she awoke.

The night alone with her had been calming but he knew that with a new day, new challenges would arise.

The attempt to escape the confines of the house without disturbing Amy turned out to be a success. He was now headed for the hospital. This time he prayed that he would not run into anyone that may be set on harming him. One of the thoughts that had crossed his mind was to report Abhorson and his allies to the King immediately then use the commotion of the ensuing battle as a distraction while he slipped into Scott's room. However, he decided this was not the best idea as Dr. Cho was involved in Abhorson's scheme. Dr. Cho's involvement would surely make the hospital an area of war while the King sent out his troops to apprehend the doctor.

Just as he had the day before, he made it to the hospital without anyone spotting him. The halls were dark and there was no moonlight coming through the windows as clouds had rolled in during the recent hours with the promise of another winter storm. Wes knew his way to Scott's room though, and without pause he continued through the darkened halls.

Scott lay just as he had before. The only difference was that he lay on top of the blankets instead of under. When he had been brought in, his shirt had been removed. No one however, had removed his pants. He still wore the same jeans that he had been wearing in the crash. Wes approached cautiously and, as he grew closer to the man's side, Scott opened his eyes.

"Are you here to kill me?" asked Scott in a whisper. He did not know who was in the room with him but he could see the outline of a man standing a few feet away from his bed in the darkness.

Wes remained silent for a moment before answering in a voice that was masked to disguise his own. "No."

"Then why have you come?"

Allowing his voice to return to normal, he answered the man who lay before him, "To find out answers."

"Wes?"

"Yeah."

"I am so sorry, this wasn't supposed to happen," Scott said in apology as he began to weep. "I ruined your life and it was too late before I realized it."

"Will you explain to me what happened?"

"I have something for you, Wes." Scott reached into the pocket of his jeans, removing an envelope as he withdrew his hand. "This will explain everything."

Wes remained still for a moment before he stepped up beside the bed to retrieve the envelope from his former friend's hand.

"Read it," Scott said in a whine.

The light in the room suddenly flickered on. Wes turned around. Standing in the doorway, a pistol in his hand, was Viktor. Wes quickly stuffed Scott's envelope in his jacket pocket to conceal it from the intruder's sight.

"You are supposed to be dead!" stammered Viktor as the realization of his failure set in.

"I suppose that is so," Wes said in the calmest manner he could muster.

Without another word Viktor fired the gun. Time froze for a split second as he waited for the bullet of the Russian's gun to rip through his flesh. The fight had been a good one but there was no way he could keep on dodging death. That's when it struck him, why wasn't he in pain? Using his hands on his body, he felt for blood. There was none. From behind a gasp of air came from the man on the bed. It was the last breath he ever took. Viktor had shot Scott, not him. Confused, he stared at the gun man.

"As far as Abhorson knows, you're dead. I like you so I am giving you a chance to run. Just remember that you will not receive a chance like this again."

"Thank you," Wes replied. The next few moments took him by complete surprise. It would be an image that would haunt him to his death. Not for the graphicness but for the lack of understanding as to why it happened.

Viktor closed his eyes, put the gun to his head and pulled the trigger. Wes watched as the man's body slumped to the floor in front of him, the wall behind where the man was just standing was painted in red. Wes just stood staring at the scene. He could have remained standing there wondering forever if it were not for the voices he heard yelling as someone came in through the entrance to the hospital. The sound of the gunshots must have drawn the attention of someone in the area. Quickly he hurried across the hall to another room. Closing the door behind him he leaned against it, letting his back slide down its surface until he was sitting on the floor. Why would Viktor kill himself and how would this affect Abhorson's plan? Maybe Viktor realized that he would go to the King and report him. A bullet to the head would surely be better than whatever grotesque punishment the King would come up with.

Outside the door he could now hear a number of voices however he could not make out what any of them were saying. There was too much commotion going on with the arrival of the help who gasped at the horrific scene they witnessed as they entered. Although words were not audible he heard the distinct sound of someone hurling at the sight of the dead bodies, which would only add to the mess.

Assuming that the cleanup would take a while he decided he would try the window to see if he could climb out and make his escape. To his luck, he found that the window opened just enough for him to slip his body through. The snow was deep behind the hospital where no one ever went and it would be easy to see his tracks as he had to literally wade through the accumulation. Not that it would matter; the only way he could be tracked was if someone actually saw him making the tracks.

With everything that was going on he thought it best not go straight over to the King's office. He would be tied up in the deaths at the hospital. The best thing he could do at the moment was head back to the house, hopefully arriving before Amy had a chance to realize he was gone.

When he entered the house, Amy was making coffee. She must have brought the coffee with her as he had searched the cupboards previously and had been unable to find any. It was obvious she had not yet heard of the killings because she appeared to be in a very bright mood.

Looking at him when he entered, she asked "Where were you?"

"I went for a walk" he replied, he was not lying. He would never actually lie to her, just skimp on the truth a little bit.

"Oh, well, I am making coffee. Would you like some?"

"Sure" he paused to inhale the aroma of the brewing drink. "May I ask you a question?"

"Of course."

"Where does all the food come from? I mean, I know there is an ice road, but I have yet to see any vehicle come in on it and in the summer there is no road."

"Well, there is a little airport a short ways past the mansion. We get a weekly flight that brings us supplies and such."

"That explains a lot…are you not supposed to be working today?"

"Actually, it is my day off."

"Well, what are your plans for the day then, Miss Kale?" he asked, moving closer to her in order to wrap his arms around her."

"I plan to celebrate."

"Celebrate what?"

"Today is my birthday!"

"That's wonderful! We must dance in celebration!" he said in a goofy way as he took a step back and offered Amy his hand. She took it and while the coffee continued to brew, they danced. There was no music to serenade them so they danced to the beat of their souls. Not once were either of them out of step with one another. It was as if they were meant to be there at that very moment in each other's arms dancing the morning away.

Wes could have danced with Amy into eternity but the cruel existence that Uranium City provided would not allow moments of happiness to thrive for long. Her radio began to come to life. It was the King's voice on the other end.

"Through the static Wes heard King say, "Miss Kale, where are you?"

She stopped dancing and went over to the counter where her radio sat. Speaking into it she said, "Just out for a morning walk. What's going on?"

"I need you to come to my office. See if you can find Mr. Petersen and bring him with you."

"I will see you shortly," she replied as she set down her radio where it had sat moments before. "So much for a day off."

"At least we can spend it together," Wes piped up, trying to be cheerful about the situation. "What do you think it is about?"

"I don't know but I am sure it can't be good, he never asks me to work on my birthday."

"Why don't I pour us each a cup of coffee? We should have time to enjoy it since you're supposed to be looking for me right now," he said with a slight laugh.

Wes went over to the counter and poured two cups of the fresh coffee. He did not care for the stuff back in the real world but it sure was a nice treat in this place. He carried the beverages over to the table where Amy had taken a seat and the two of them sat there silently as they sipped on the coffee, both of them lost in thought about their own fears as to why the King would call upon them so randomly.

When the drink was finished they left the little house. Amy had walked over the day before but the snowmobile he had stashed was still parked out of sight behind the building. When Wes reminded her of this she went directly to it and fired it up.

While he waited he looked up into the sky. The clouds looked even more menacing now that it was daylight. A few snowflakes were beginning to fall and there was no doubt in his mind this storm was going to be destructive. The sky's hold on him was broken when Amy pulled up in front of him on the sled.

"Are you ready?" she asked.

"As ready as I ever will be," was all he could muster up as a reply. Climbing on behind her they took off with their direction set for the King's office. In the short amount of time they were traveling, the amount of snow descending from the clouds had drastically increased.

The hall leading to the office of the King was silent. Everyone was most likely off dealing with the events that had transpired earlier in the morning. Amy knocked lightly on the King's door. It had been left slightly open and the pressure from her hand widened the opening allowing a view of the King who sat behind his desk in disarray. The King's hair was wild, strands shooting off in all directions as if the man had just been electrocuted. This surprised Wes as the King was normally very well presented.

"Oh, hello. Please come in," said the King, moving his hand in a waving motion. "I wanted to ask a favor of you two."

"What can we do for you?" asked Amy before Wes had a chance to even speak.

"There is unrest amongst the prisoners. As I am sure you both know by now, someone committed arson on the library. It is sad because it was there for the benefit of our population. However this is not the only horrendous act committed in recent hours. This morning an individual walked into the hospital and shot the survivor of the plane crash before taking his own life." The King paused for a minute allowing the information he had just provided to sink into his audience. "I am not sure how this man came into possession of the weapon but it really does not matter. What matters is that somehow the prisoners of this great place have gained access to the tools of destruction that have brought a number of them here." Another pause, "I am having my annual party for my financial contributors in three days and I wish to ask the two of you to attend the party disguised as guests in case anything goes wrong. You would not be alone of course, I will have guards close by in the event they are needed but I do not wish to have my guests burdened with the worry of seeing armed guards all around my home during the occasion."

"I would be happy to," announced Amy.

"And what about you, Mr. Petersen?" the King asked, switching his gaze from Amy to him.

"Anything you need, sir."

"Wonderful, I am so grateful to have you both on my side. Now, Miss Kale, you may take Mr. Petersen home then enjoy the rest of your day since it is your birthday."

"Thank you," she acknowledged as she gave Wes a nudge towards the door.

He took in a breath of contempt; he hated that the King assumed he was on his side. He may be playing favor to the King but he was on his own side. He would figure out a way for him and Amy to escape the grasps of the evil man who hid behind that enormous desk in his office.

Walking down the hall away from the meeting he and Amy just had, his mind was racing. He already had an idea about the party, but three days was very soon. Things were going to start moving at a very fast pace. Three days meant that he had to develop a plan, and fast. According to the conversation he had overheard, Abhorson's attack was to take place during the annual party. No matter who won this fight the best chance at escaping would be during the raid on the mansion. Timing would be crucial in order to achieve success. The other problem was Amy; would it be best to include her in the plan or just wait until the moment, whisking her away with him at the very last second? Deciding on the latter of the two options he kept his thoughts to himself as they approached the snowmobile that was waiting out front where they had left it upon arriving.

The storm continued to increase in velocity as they rode back to the house. Conditions had become almost blinding. It was a true whiteout. When Amy brought the snowmobile to a stop outside the house he could not even see an outline of the building even though they were only parked about fifteen feet away.

"Why don't you go inside?" she suggested to him. "I am going to go get us some food."

"Sounds good," he replied but the sound of his voice was drowned out by the howl of the wind forcing him to repeat himself in more of a yell.

He trudged towards the direction he knew the house to be in. The snow was already drifting up against the door and it took all his strength to be able to pull it open enough for him to slip into its sheltering comfort. Listening, he heard the roar of the snowmobile's engine die off as it gained distance. There was nothing left to do but wait for Amy's return.

Chapter 13

Wes waited for three hours but Amy failed to return. During that time the storm had only worsened and he began to think that maybe she had to stop and take shelter from its brutality. There was, after all, no way for them to communicate, so that was the situation he hoped for. When he was sure that Amy would not make it back with food he checked the refrigerator. Sure enough she had brought some food with her when she had come over the day before, not much but it was enough to concoct some sort of a meal. He ate two apples and a slice of a banana loaf, these were his only options. Just after finishing his meal, the power went out and there was nothing left to do but sit in the dark. After a while he decided he may as well go to bed and get some rest for he had a hunch that, in the following days, sleep may become a luxury.

Several hours of undisturbed sleep filled Wes's night until it was interrupted by a knock on the front door. The power was still out, forcing him to fumble his way through the darkness. Assuming it was Amy outside he pushed open the door. Snow was still swirling through the air. Standing on the small porch was an individual wearing a hooded cloak. In his hand he carried a lantern that did not do much more than cast eerie shadows in the winter's wrath. Looking at the lamp he immediately recognized it to be some sort of miner's light. He had seen them a few times before in the hands of prisoners when they had emerged from the depths of the mines at the end of their work days.

"Aren't you gonna invite me in?" asked the man standing outside as he raised the lantern allowing a small amount of the light to cross his face. The sight was disturbing. The man was smiling, revealing a row of rotten teeth. The light also danced across the man's eye sockets. One eye was completely missing. These features were complimented by a long scraggly grey beard.

Wes was caught by surprise and was unsure who this man was. Thinking for a moment, he decided to grant him entrance. If the man decided to try anything he was sure he would be able to defend himself in any potential fight, providing he was not armed with a gun or other weapon.

The man went directly to the table where he sat down without saying another word. Wes was extremely confused as to who this person was and why he had come.

"May I ask why you are here?"

"I have come to see you, Wes."

"I gathered that, the question is why?"

"I wanted to meet you."

"I need a better answer than that. Why would you want to meet me?"

The man coughed, a rotten tooth flying out onto the table. "You know, we met once, a long time ago." Picking up his tooth, he blew it off and proceeded to stick it in a pocket that was located on the front side of his cloak.

"I don't remember us meeting."

"Of course you don't, you were but a baby." The man waved Wes over to take a seat with him at the table.

Hesitant, he made his way over from the doorway where he still stood. Taking a seat across from his visitor, he caught a foul stench that hung around the man like an aura. "Who are you?"

"Sid," his guest replied. Once again he smiled revealing the same ugly teeth he had before only with one less this time.

"Okay, but I still don't understand why we would have met in the past? Or should I say why you would have met me when I was a baby?"

"Ah, a good question." Sid thought for a moment, "I knew your mother."

Now Wes was getting slightly angry, another person in this hell hole was bringing up his mother who had been dead for over twenty years. "Why would you know my mother?"

"Another good question... I am your father."

The old man's proclamation shocked and horrified Wes at the same time. Sitting before him was a man who had just claimed to be his father, a man who had vanished when he was just a baby. This did not seem possible, even though he had been told that his father had done time here and had escaped.

"Do you have proof?" he asked. It was the only question that he could come up with.

"I do." The man reached into the same pocket he had placed his tooth in. When he pulled his hand out, he was gripping a ragged old photo. Placing it on the table under the light cast from his lantern Sid pointed at it. "Look."

Wes stared down at the photo. It was stained and torn but he could make out a face under all the grime. It was his mother. He did not know what to do. Something seemed very off about this situation. This man looked nothing like him. At the same time, how could one explain how he had come across a picture of his mother? "But you escaped this place! Why are you here?"

"I never really escaped this place. I was too weak to attempt it. The night before I was supposed to escape, I fell down a mine shaft and broke my arm. I was trapped there for three days before I was finally able to get out. My escape partner had left without me and because I was not around for my following shifts everyone had assumed that I went with him."

"What happened after that?"

"I went about my daily business except I didn't have to work because I no longer existed. So, I converted a room in one of the abandoned buildings to be my home and I go to the dining hall for my meals. So many people go through there that they don't notice that an extra couple of meals go missing each day."

Wes was surprised at the man's story. It was growing ever more plausible. "What now?" he asked.

"Now I must ask you to do something for me, my son. I have been trying for years to get close to the King in order to get revenge for your mother's murder and now you show up and have close access. Can you kill him? In the name of your mother, of course."

There it was. This was no friendly visit. Just like everyone else in this godforsaken place, Sid had an agenda. Only this time, he felt the man's pain. For the first time he felt that he was truly capable of killing the King. "I will do it." When the words left his mouth he had no doubt that he meant what he was saying. Although his supposed father convinced him, it was solely for the sake of getting revenge for his mother that he agreed to the task that had been presented so many times before.

"Thank you, my son. Your mother would have been proud." Sid then stood up. He hugged his son as tight as his frail body would allow. "Now I must be going, the storm is starting to let up and I do not wish to be caught out wandering. One must be careful when one isn't supposed to exist."

Wes nodded as the man departed. The hug was a tad on the creepy side. When Sid was gone, relief washed over him. For years he had no family or at least no family by blood, other than his grandparents. Now he had just sat down at a table with a man claiming to be his father. Uranium city was truly a strange place. It threw curve balls that no one could ever predict.

It was only a minute or two before Wes could hear some sort of commotion going on outside. There was lots of yelling but it did sound slightly distant. Walking to the window he peered out. The storm had almost come to a stop. A little ways down the road stood Sid. He was arguing with two guards. In an instant, things went bad. Sid reached into his pocket and pulled out a knife. It looked as if the guards were trying to reason with him but when Sid lunged forward at one of the guards it left no choice for the other guard except to shoot in an attempt to protect his comrade. Sid and his knife crashed to the ground, his cloak settling around him like a large blanket. The entire act was lit up by the lantern which he must have sat on the ground when he encountered the patrol. Wes felt no remorse or anger about this death. He had only just met the man after all. Maybe he was even becoming desensitized, having to survive in this horrible place. Without another thought he returned to his bedroom. The power was still out and Sid's lantern now sat out in the snow a few paces from where his body fell for the final time.

Sleep did not come easy as he lay in his unlit room. He listened to what was around him but the only sound was the beating of his own heart. Daylight still remained far in the future, a future that was very unsure. Sid's visit had done much damage to the plan that had previously begun to take shape in his mind. Now things had to be rewritten. The King had to die and he was going to do it, of that there was no doubt in his mind. The question was when? With a little more thought he established the idea to kill the King at the party. After the deed was done he and Amy could run away. No more would the King keep either of them locked away in Uranium City Prison.

Chapter 14

Upon morning light, Wes remained in bed. Out the window he could see that the snow was no longer falling. Amy had failed to return and the man claiming to be his father, was dead. The hours of darkness had been long and drawn out, with little sleep. He wondered what would be in store on this day. How could the previous days in Uranium City be outdone? After lying in bed for the majority of the morning, he decided to go out and fetch some breakfast at the dining hall. His dinner the night before had been skimpy at best and the hunger he felt was starting to gnaw away at him.

Leaving the house on this morning, he felt slightly anxious. He prayed that the body of his father had been disposed of and not left in the middle of the road as he did not feel that he could stomach having to walk by it on his way to get something to eat. On the stroll towards his destination, thoughts of the party that was to take place on the following evening played through his mind. It seemed so close, yet so far away. Each day passed by slowly but he could not believe that he had already been here for as long as he had. Much had happened in that short amount of time and so much more would happen in the days to come.

To his relief, Sid's body had been removed from where it had fallen limp the night before. Although there was no evidence that the man had died on that very spot only a few hours previously, when Wes walked by he did feel pity for the fellow. Pity was not enough though, there was a desire to feel more but he did not know the man and was unable to conjure up the feelings. The only contribution the man ever had given him was convincing him that killing the King would be justified in the name of his mother. Anger brewed deep within his soul as he continued his walk, only subsiding when he reached the dining hall.

Entering the building, the smell of home cooking curled up his nostrils. It was a great feeling to sit down at a table with a plate of scrambled eggs and hash browns after a night such as the one he just had. The taste may have been mediocre at best but you couldn't beat the satisfaction that a warm room and a full stomach could give a man.

When he was finished with his meal, he was unsure as to what he should do next. Then he started to wonder what had happened to Amy. Why had she not returned? Where was she? These were questions that needed answers so, with nothing else on his plate for the day he set out to find them.

Wes did not have to travel far before he found what he was looking for. Shortly after he left the hall Amy rolled up beside him in her pickup truck.

"Get in." she said through her partly rolled down window.

He did as he was told, climbing into the passenger seat. "Where have you been?"

"I went home to grab some stuff, the storm just got too bad for me to return." She answered as she pulled the truck away from the temporary parking space it had taken when she stopped to pick up her companion.

"I thought you would have stopped by this morning."

"I was not able to. I had to do some work, the guards had to shoot one of the prisoners last night and arrangements for disposal of the body had to be made."

He nodded to her in understanding. He remained silent though, wishing to keep the true identity of the deceased to himself. Even if he did want to share the information with her, there was no way to be one hundred percent sure that the man had been telling the truth anyways. For all he knew, Abhorson could have sent an imposter to manipulate him into killing the King. "Where are we headed?"

"Mr. King had a few tuxedos flown in last night, he wants you to try them on and then pick one to wear to tomorrow night's ball."

"You know, I have never had to wear a tuxedo before. It is kind of exciting."

"Is that so?" replied a grinning Amy.

"What about you? Did Mr. King get you anything fancy?"

"Matter of fact, he did. I even got to choose my dress straight from a catalogue."

"Aren't you special?" he said, poking fun at Amy, only it did not have the reaction he had hoped for. She turned her head away as if he had slapped her. Somehow he had thrown a great insult without even knowing how. "I'm sorry," he apologized, trying to back pedal the hurt he had caused with his smart ass remark.

"It's okay," she said, bringing a false smile to her face.

She pulled up in front of the old high school that housed the King's office.

"What are we doing here?" asked Wes, confused.

"You are going to try on your tux."

"Here, at Mr. King's office?"

Laughing, she said "This is a large building. It houses many things other than just Mr. King's office."

Leading the way, Amy had Wes follow her to a large room towards the rear of the building. The room appeared as if it had been the gym at some point in history. Now there where tables set up throughout the area and he assumed it might have been used as some kind of assembly room for the prison guards. To the left were two separate doors that looked like change rooms. His assumption was confirmed when Amy pointed at them and told him the attire he was to try on was located inside the one on the right.

"Make sure you come out and show me how it looks when you pick one," she called as she took a seat at one of the tables and watched him head for the change room.

He entered the room. It looked like any typical gym change room that one might find in a school. Nothing had been altered so the room could operate as something else, unlike the rest of the rooms he had noticed in the building. Hanging on hooks that lined the wall were five different tuxedos that he could choose from. All of them were black except for one, which happened to be white. For some reason he felt drawn to the white tuxedo. He removed it from the hook on the wall and began to undress so that he could try it on. Once he was dressed he looked into a mirror that still remained in the room. If it was not for his pale skin and now patchy hair, he could have passed as someone who was rich and famous.

The white tux fit perfectly. He made the decision that he did not need to try on the others, this was the one he wanted to wear.

With the verdict decided he went out to show himself off to Amy.

She was still seated where she had been before. A book was in her hands, one of the very few that he imagined still remained in the prison after the library burnt to the ground. When she took notice of his presence she set the book down to focus her attention on him.

He smiled as he turned to the side and raised his hand like a gun, giving her a James Bond styled pose. She laughed and gave a slight clap but then she remembered where they were and forced herself to regain a more serious composure.

"It suits you, Mr. Petersen," she said while giving a quick wink.

"Why, thank you."

"Now we need to do something with your hair."

"My hair?"

"Yes, that god awful mess on your head," she attempted to say in a British accent, trying to be funny. She was far from successful at accomplishing the accent but her effort was quite comical.

"Can anything be done to save it?" Wes replied in his own poorly constructed British accent, only he was much more successful at conveying the tone.

They both chuckled over the childishness of their conversation. She then led him to the staff barber who happened to have set up shop in one of the old classrooms. Wes knew the prisoners also had a barber set up in one of the old buildings by the town center, however, he assumed that the employee barber was much more qualified. The King was the type of person who would never allow an amateur to touch his hair, he was quite sure of that.

When they arrived at the room where the barber practiced his art, they found him there eating some lunch. The man was a short, overweight, bald fellow with a funny little goatee. He welcomed Amy with a hug before looking over at his challenge and shaking his head.

"I am Phillip, the greatest barber in the country!" the little man said, introducing himself.

"I am Wes."

"I know that, you silly man. Now sit down and let me see what kind of magic I can work."

Wes did as he was told taking a seat in the chair that was located in front of a big mirror. Phillip began to look over the canvas before him. He moved around Wes to take him in from all different angles. During the process the man mumbled to himself and Wes could never quite make out what the funny little man was saying except for the odd thing here and there like "No, no" and "This will never work". Finally, Phillip stopped bustling around and announced, "I am afraid there is only one option. The hair is just too damaged to work with. He must go bald like the great Phillip."

Wes cringed, he was not sure if it was because the man cutting his hair referred to himself in the third person or if it was the fact that the only option to look presentable was to be completely bald. Deep down, he knew that Phillip's choice was the only option. He had looked in the mirror and saw the mess that lay atop his head. But going bald was not really going to help him much as he still had large amounts of scabbing on his scalp from when he had been hit with the pickaxe in the mine.

Phillip wrapped a barber's cape around him so he wouldn't get any hair on the tux that he was still wearing. It only took a minute for the hair to be completely gone from his head. Looking in the mirror he noticed that he looked very badass with no hair. Phillip removed the cape, freeing Wes from the chair so that he could move on to the next stage of his day.

"Looks good," complimented Amy. "Now we must go see Mr. King, he wants to see you.

"Okay," answered Wes.

He continued on to the King's office with Amy. The office door was wide open for the first time that he had ever seen. Inside the King sat behind his desk. He was in a much more presentable state than he had been the day before. He even looked as if he had also paid a visit to Phillip, possibly earlier that morning.

"Welcome!" declared the King when they entered the room.

"You wanted to see me, sir?" asked Wes.

"Yes, I wanted to talk to you about the party tomorrow."

"Okay."

"I just wanted to give a few instructions. One, you are a guest so please feel free to mingle and partake in the activities. I don't want the other guests to be suspicious of you. Two, if one of the other guests asks who you are just inform them that you are a personal friend who is involved in some mutual investments with me. Three, if something does go wrong, deal with the problem immediately. However, you are only to deal with problems at the mansion and anything that may happen in the prison will be dealt with by the guards here. Under no circumstances are you to leave the party, it would put my guests at risk. Understand?"

"Yes," he answered.

"Good…by the way, I have a gift for you." The King rose from his seat and walked over to one of the large wall cabinets in the office. "I know you may be a little self-conscious about your head wound so I want you to have this to wear to the ball tomorrow night. It will go great with your choice of attire." The King removed a top hat from the cabinet and, walking back towards his desk he handed it to Wes. "Put it on," the King directed as he retook his seat.

Wes did as he was ordered.

"Now, what do you think, Miss Kale, does he not look great?"

"I think he looks elegant."

"Perfect!" announced the King. "Mr. Petersen, I want you to go back to the change rooms and put your other clothes back on. Someone will bring the tuxedo and hat up to the house later today, then at three o-clock tomorrow afternoon Miss Kale will pick you up and bring you to my home where there will be a little more preparation. Make sure you are dressed and ready to go when Miss Kale arrives. I expect both of you to be punctual."

"Of course," Wes answered before turning away and heading back to change into his other clothes.

Amy remained in the office after he left, leaving him alone to navigate his way back to the change room. Luckily it was a fairly simple path, down to the end of the hall and to the right. After changing he hung the tux back on the wall where he had got it from earlier; he also placed the top hat with it. Once dressed he went back to find Amy but she had left and gone somewhere with the truck leaving him to make the trek back to the house on his own.

Wes made the short journey to his house. He had nothing left to do and was tired so he waited for the person to bring him his party clothes and , once they had come and gone, he crawled into bed hoping that it would be the last night he would spend trapped in the Hell known as Uranium City.

The following day was the big one. It was inevitable that Uranium City Prison would never be the same after. Whether it would be for the good or the bad Wes did not know. He just made sure to prepare his mind for the deed that needed to be done. There was no way to plan every detail as he did not know how things were going to play out at the party. The only sure thing was that he would wait until chaos broke loose on the guests. It would provide the perfect cover for him to enact his mother's revenge. When the deed was done he would find Amy and they would attempt to escape together.

Chapter 15

A new day beckoned as Wes rose with the sun. It was to be a day of action. He had nothing to do until that afternoon but much was on his mind. Food was something that would be needed as he was sure he would require the energy that a hearty meal would provide. He got dressed and left for the dining hall. It was sure to be busy at this time of day but that would work to his advantage. With any luck he would go unnoticed by his enemies.

Upon arriving at the hall something seemed out of place. Things were very quiet. The last time he had come at this time of day there were prisoners bustling around everywhere. The weather was not overly bad, cold yes, but the skies were clear and no wind dared to blow. This ruled out nature as the driving force keeping everyone away.

Opening the door to the hall he found the interior to be nearly empty. A few men were spread out here and there amongst the tables. "The calm before the storm," he whispered to himself. Moving his mind past the peculiar lack of people he made his way over to the counter to collect his plate of food.

On this morning the food tasted magnificent. There was nothing different about it but it was possible the change in taste was a mental result of him knowing this could very well be the last meal he would ever have to eat in the UCP dining hall.

With his meal finished he walked back to the house one final time. He was growing anxious about the escape. Although he still didn't know quite what the plan was going to be, getting out of the prison was the easy task. Making it to civilization would not be a simple accomplishment. On his way back he took his time. He passed where the library once stood, stopping to stare at it for a moment. The burnt out bus still remained entangled among the debris and that got him thinking about the masked individual. He wondered if he ever would find out who had helped keep him alive during his time spent in the prison. Shrugging it off and deciding it was best to remain unknown, he continued on. A small detour led him to the front entrance of the hospital. He had no intention of entering but he did stand staring for a moment at the building that looked uninhabited on this morning. Closing his eyes he prayed that Scott may rest in peace.

With nowhere else he particularly wanted to see he arrived back at the little house that had been designated as his home. Going inside he decided to have a soak in the tub before dressing for the party. The water was comforting. It helped to relax him, allowing his mind to free itself from its burdens. He spent nearly an hour in the water, every time it started to get cold he would drain a little of the tub's contents so he could top it up with fresh hot liquid.

When it was time to get out of the bath he began to dress in the tuxedo the King had provided for him to wear to the party. Just like the day before it was as if he transformed in front of the mirror. He went from being a dirty, grimy prisoner to a movie star. The white tux gleamed and when he placed the top hat on his head it appeared as if he was no longer himself. He really did feel like he was some movie hero. All dressed up in fancy clothes with a secret plot to kill the bad guy at a party how could he not feel like James Bond? The only thing he needed was a gun but he had a feeling that if the King trusted him enough to help guard the party he would be provided with one.

There was a knock on the door. It was nearly three and he knew it was Amy picking him up to take him to the King's ball. Going to the door he opened it up. Standing before him was Amy in the most amazing red dress he had ever seen. It made her look more beautiful than ever. She even carried in her hand a small matching red purse.

"Wow!" was all he could muster to say after laying his eyes on his date.

"I should say the same about you, Mr. Petersen. Now, are you ready to escort me to the party?"

"I am," he replied, taking her arm in his and stepping off the porch with her. Wes had his coat tucked under his other arm just in case the weather grew colder. When they were about halfway down the path he finally looked away from his companion. That was when he saw what she had arrived in. She had somehow been able to get her hands on the King's prized car, only this time its beauty did not compare to the woman on his arm. "I thought Mr. King did not allow anyone to touch his car?"

"I was persuasive," she said while giving a quick wink.

"Can I drive it?"

"No way in hell!" she exclaimed, following her words with a slight giggle.

Wes was okay with that, he would have been happy no matter what transportation he had to take as long as Amy was by his side. She got into the driver's seat carefully so she didn't wrinkle her dress. He did the same when getting into the passenger seat as he did not dare mess up his attire.

The ride to the mansion was enjoyable. There were no words spoken, none were needed. A smile remained on Amy's face the entire trip. One also spent a lot of time on Wes's face but it faded for a moment when he started to think about the evening's activities.

Amy pulled the car up in front of the mansion, parking it close to the doors. There were also three limos out front. Wes wondered if the King kept them at the airport for when he brought in important guests and came to the conclusion that he must because he would not dare to hire cars to come up here on the ice road. Doing so would expose his whole operation. With that assumption Wes made another. The King must also have some of his other guards act as drivers to go back and forth to the small private airport Amy had told him about.

Wes followed Amy into the King's home. He recognized a couple of the King's employees who he had seen around the prison on prior occasions. They were moving around carrying cases of wine and platters of food, obviously in preparation for the evening's guests. Amy led him to a room down one of the main halls. It was not a large room but it did not need to be. It was designed to be a small office. He did not imagine that it was one that the King actually used. Closing the door behind her, she kissed him then proceeded to go to the desk where she withdrew two guns from the drawer. Both were small pistols. She handed one to Wes, putting the other in her purse.

"You remember how to use that thing, correct?"

"Of course, you taught me well," he smiled.

"Good…now I have a couple things that I need to attend to." She moved over to the window and looked out. "The limos are gone which means that the guests will be arriving shortly. Go eat some food and mingle with the others when they arrive." She started to leave then paused and turned back to him to mention one final thing. "I will find you after and I expect a dance." With that said she exited the room.

He was standing all alone in the small office. He longed to spend the entire evening with Amy however he knew that was not the reason he was here. He had been brought in order to watch over things in case Abhorson made a move, which the man was sure to do. The question was when. Wes took his time heading back down the hall towards the main room. As he walked he admired the many paintings that lined the walls, all of which he was sure cost a small fortune. The gun Amy had given him was tucked inside his tuxedo jacket, hooked into a small holster-type thing that had been sewn in. It had not been there the day before when he had originally tried the garment it on.

Inside the great room he found a table that was already lined with variety of food and beverages. He causally took a piece off a meat tray and ate it then poured himself a small glass of champagne. He knew he should not be drinking this night but what harm could one glass cause?

Wes had yet to see the host of the evening. He imagined the King would wait for everyone to arrive then make some sort of grand entrance. That was just the kind of person the King was. There was nothing left for him to do except admire the architecture while he waited. After about fifteen minutes he found himself back at the tables looking for another snack. This time he was able to refrain from indulging in any more of the exquisite champagne.

Soon after his snack the guests began to arrive. A group of about ten people came through the doors. They were all dressed elegantly, the men in tuxedos and the women in dresses just as he and Amy had been outfitted. Once the first group arrived it was just the start of things. More and more people began to show up. The place was starting to liven as people mingled and began to snack on the provided food. Wes wandered around the room among the crowd that had accumulated. A few brief conversations were all he was able to muster. The class difference between himself and the

King's guests was so large that he had no idea how to carry on a conversation when someone would mention their yacht or other fine luxury item then ask him if he ever considered buying one. He tried to remain inconspicuous but it was difficult. Every word that came out of his mouth was a blatant lie. Then again, how could it not be? The King would have him hanged if he were to tell the truth about himself. He wondered where Amy was. She was the only one he could be honest with. She had yet to show herself since leaving him alone after handing over the gun.

At about six-thirty the band arrived and immediately began to play. Their specialty was swing, it was as if the King had reached into the nineteen-thirties and plucked the band from time. One of the female members even did vocals and her voice was dead on with that style of music. Once the sound of instruments and singing filled the air the guest's feet began to dance to the beat. The great room offered ample space for such a thing. It was about seven when the King finally decided to grace everyone with his presence. Just as Wes suspected he made sure he was the focal point of the room when he entered. The band stopped playing, all the guests freezing in place as they turned their attention to the top of the grand staircase where the King stood for all to see. No one dared to make a sound. The evening's help began to hand out glasses of champagne as they walked through the crowd, platters in hand with many crystal glasses twinkling in the light cast from the excessive amount of chandeliers that lined the well-constructed ceiling.

"Welcome!" bellowed the King. "I hope you are all enjoying the evening's festivities. This is my gift to you for your continued support." The King raised his own crystal glass in the air. "I would like to make a toast to another successful year for us all!"

Everyone drank to the King's little speech, including Wes. Amy was still nowhere to be found. It slightly bothered him since he needed to know where she was if he was going to make everything fall into place during the course of the night. He thought he heard the crack of gunfire going off somewhere distant from the mansion. Before he could focus his hearing on what was causing the noise the music once again began to play. His eyes darted to the King who was making his way down the steps to join his guests in the celebration.

Thinking that the sounds he had heard must have been gunfire, Wes was bothered. It meant that things were now in motion. Uranium City Prison was under revolt and it would only be a matter of time before the violence would reach the mansion's doors. He wanted to be long gone before that time came but he could not deal with the King in the open. He had to wait for him to leave the room at some point, that's when he would follow him until they were alone then he would make his move.

He continued to move around throughout the crowd having brief conversations with more of the party goers, but he never strayed far from the King. He wanted to keep his target in sight so he would know to follow when the time came. At a few minutes past eight Amy appeared. The atmosphere in the room made her appear even more beautiful than earlier. She immediately made her way over to Wes.

"Care to dance?" she asked as she approached.

"I would love too, my lady!" he replied, taking her hand in his and leading her out onto the dance floor.

As they danced to the music he felt as rich and powerful as anyone else in the room just by having her in his arms. But he could not allow himself to get too caught up in the moment and he kept one eye on the King at all times. About halfway through the second song since Amy had arrived the King finally exited the room.

"I have to go to the washroom," Wes whispered in Amy's ear as they continued to dance. "I will be right back." He hated to lie to her and hated even more the look on her face as he left her standing alone in the middle of the dance floor, the other guests still twirling around her.

Wes made haste, yet kept his pace slow enough that he would not draw attention to himself. He knew which hall the King had gone down but hoped that he would be able to spot him when he rounded the corner before the man disappeared into another room. He entered the hallway just in time to watch as the King stepped through a door a few paces down on the left. Looking behind him he saw that he was alone in the hall then jogged the rest of the way to the room the King had entered.

The door the King had gone through was closed. Taking a deep breath Wes turned the knob. Before he could push the door open gunshots rang out in room he had just left. Abhorson's army must have arrived. Following the first blast of gunfire were the screams of the party's guests. The Band's music immediately came to a stop as another burst of gunfire rang out. People were now spilling into the hall in an attempt to escape the bloodshed that was taking place in the great room. Although Amy's safety concerned him, he knew she could take care of herself in the chaos. Wes pushed his way through the door, closing it behind him.

Looking around the room he took in his surroundings. It was a library, not like the one that had burnt down however. This was a library that housed rare books. He was not an expert but just by looking at the bindings he could tell that many of the books were very old.

Turning his attention back to the task set in his mind he saw the King. He was seated in a chair by a large brick fireplace. A picture frame was in his hand. Wes was unable to see what it contained from across the room but when he looked into the King's eyes. It looked as if the man before him was crying.

"You don't have to tell me, Mr. Petersen. I can hear the gunfire in the other room. There is nothing we can do now. In about four minutes this room will seal itself for a period of twenty four hours. It is a custom designed security system."

"What about all your guests?"

"They will probably die."

"That's horrible! How can you let your friends die?" an astonished Wes asked.

"They are no more than business acquaintances. There are more where they came from." The King paused, "You are welcome to wait this out with me."

"I have a better idea," Wes retorted, disgusted with what he had heard just come out of the King's mouth. The man had no respect for anyone but himself and he was willing to let a mass killing take place just down the hall without a care in the world. He removed the pistol Amy had given him from his coat, and aiming it at the King asked, "Any last words?"

"No, I am ready to die. It is actually quite perfect. Sixteen years ago today my wife died. She is the one in this picture," the King said, holding the photo up for him to see. The woman in the picture was quite attractive, what she ever saw in the King was to be questioned.

Caught off guard Wes almost felt sorry for the man. He then remembered his mother and how she was dead and how it was his fault. He stared at the King as he took a deep breath and planted his feet before taking the shot.

The door flew open just as he was about to fire. He looked back. Amy was standing in the doorway her own pistol pointed but her target was different than his. She had the gun aimed directly towards him.

"I can't let you do this, Wes!" she cried.

"But he killed my mother and he has been holding you here," argued Wes.

"That may be so, but you are not a killer, Wes. I could never forgive myself if I let you kill him."

"I need to do it," he argued.

"You can't!" she screamed back at him, now in tears herself.

Emotions were filling his head. He did not know what to do. He felt that he needed to kill the King. It was the only way to make things fair. "Why?" he asked, thinking there had to be a stronger reason why she would not allow it. He just did not believe it was simply that she did not want him to have the King's death on his conscience. If that were all, she would not be pointing her own gun at him.

"Because he is my father!" she admitted with a sob.

Wes was horrified at the information he had just learned. It explained so much and yet he had trouble believing the two could be related. He knew he could no longer accomplish the task he had set out to do. He loved her and knew that if he were to kill the King she would never forgive him. With that, he lowered his gun.

"But your last name is different," he stated while looking into her eyes. He knew she was telling the truth and was simply grasping at the last straw of making the truth not so.

"My mother's... Quick, we must escape. Follow me." she instructed.

Wes reluctantly did as he was told. He wanted to stay in defiance. She had failed to tell him who she was all along. Deep down though, he knew this was his only chance at survival. Even if her father was evil, he loved her and would forgive her in the end. They would escape together. As they entered the hallway once again the sound of gunfire and screams were still resounding strong in the air. Several bodies were already in the hall. It looked as if they had been injured then attempted to drag themselves down the hall away from any further harm but had succumbed to their injuries.

"We will go out the side door!" Amy called back to Wes who was trailing behind her. How she was able to run in the dress she was wearing he did not know. He was having trouble in the tuxedo. Continuing to lead the way she took him through several rooms before they came to an exit that came out into a garden that looked to have the potential to be a marvel in the summer months.

Sneaking around the outside wall of the house they stayed close in order to remain in the shadows. Arriving at the front driveway there was a mess of gore. Just like it was inside, bodies were spread out in the front yard of the mansion. Wes looked to the treeline where he saw one of the men he had talked to during the party. The man was running away from the house. He had almost made it into the cover of the forest but a bullet tore through the suit he wore.

He recognized Fritz standing on the front porch of the home. He had a rifle in his hand and was just lowering it after shooting the man who had been escaping when Wes had spotted him. Before he could point him out, Amy had already noticed him and fired two rounds from her pistol into his chest. Fritz dropped to the ground, dying instantly.

The King's car was just a short distance away. Amy made a break for it, Wes hot on her heels. They were able to get in and drive off before anyone else came outside and noticed. He had questions about the King but knew it was a subject that would forever be off limits.

"Where are we going?" he asked as she drove down the road.

"To the airport, there will be a couple of helicopters there along with the pilots. The pilots are instructed to fly guests to and from a small place called Fort Smith. If we can get to the airstrip we will be home free."

This was the greatest news he had received since before he had come to Uranium City Prison. He was finally going to leave what really was the end of the line for many, and Amy was going to go with him.

Chapter 16

The car traveled a long way before it sputtered as the engine died. The King's prized possession slowly rolled to a stop in the middle of the road. Wes looked at Amy in alarm. He was wondering how far they would have to walk up the road before they reached the airstrip.

"It is out of gas," announced Amy.

"How much further do we have to go?"

"No too far, it is only about a mile from here," she answered as she climbed out of the automobile.

Wes followed suit. He was about to close the door behind him when he remembered his coat. Reaching back in, he grabbed it along with another one that his companion must have left in the backseat earlier in the night. He handed Amy her coat before putting his own on. Looking ahead he cringed. The only light they had available to lead the way was the glowing of the moon and it was playing hide and seek behind the clouds. Even with unfavorable conditions they trudged on towards their destination. It was closer than going back and in this situation there was nothing to return to anyways.

After a fair amount of walking, more than either of them had been prepared to do, they rounded the final bend in the road. Several helicopters could be seen resting in front of a large airplane hangar. Wes almost wanted to run but his feet were frozen from tramping through the snow. Escape was so close that he could almost touch it however Uranium City Prison was not going to give up that easily. Out from the shadows stepped a familiar figure.

Abhorson walked to the center of the road about twenty feet from where they stood, the old man's cane being the dead giveaway as to who was crossing their path.

"How was the party?" the old man asked, chuckling as if it was the funniest question in the world.

"Eventful," Wes answered in a bitter voice.

"Word is that you didn't kill the King." Abhorson began to walk towards them as he talked. "I really thought that old bastard I sent to pretend to be your father would work." He was growing closer, now only a few paces away. "You have disappointed me once again!"

Wes was in shock. So much deceit had befallen him in recent times he was unsure what to believe anymore. "What do you want? You have succeeded in taking the prison, just let us go!"

"That may be so but we have unfinished business. I had hoped that we could do this together but, you betrayed me and now you must suffer the consequences!" Abhorson raised his left arm as the moon's light revealed itself from behind one of its hiding places. The glow danced off something shiny in the old man's hand. By the time Wes realized what it was, it was too late. The gunshot rang out into the air. Time slowed to a crawl as he waited for the bullet to penetrate his flesh.

It was the scream that brought him back to reality. He turned to face Amy as she placed her hands on her stomach. Her red dress was slowly darkening in color and she fell to her knees. Blood was already starting to appear at the corners of her lips. He rushed to her side as she collapsed into the snow. A final gasp of air was all she could muster before death whisked her away. Wes wrapped his arms around her and began to weep wishing that it was him lying in the snow instead. Her parting caused more pain than he thought a human could ever suffer.

"You should have known better than to mess with me! I am Abhorson! Do you know where that name comes from?" The old man waited for a reply but his victim just continued to sob on the ground as he held the woman's body in his arms. "Abhorson was the executioner in one of Shakespeare's works. I have killed more men than you could imagine. You should feel lucky that I am sparing your life, Wes." The man turned away and began to hobble on his cane towards the prison's airport.

Amy's little red purse caught Wes's attention. He had left the pistol he was given in the car but remembered that she had placed hers back in her handbag. He reached over and removed the gun. Looking down the sights he took a deep breath as he aimed, just as Amy had taught him to do. As he exhaled he pulled the trigger. The shot echoed through the air as the bullet sought out its target. Abhorson dropped to the ground. He could hear the old man groaning in pain, the shot had failed to kill him.

When he had reached into the purse he had felt something else in it. Out of curiosity he reached back in to find out what Amy had carried with her to her death. It was the black book, the one that the masked individual had used to communicate with him. Holding it in his hand for a moment and thinking about what this discovery meant he then stuck the book back in the purse.

The roar of an engine could be heard off in the distance. He knew he had to leave now before anyone showed up and compromised his escape. He hated to leave Amy behind lying alone in the snow but there was nothing he could do about it so he made his way over to where the helicopters were waiting. One pilot stood outside his aircraft. He was mesmerized by what he had just witnessed. Wes yelled at him to get the engine started and it brought the man back to reality. He did as he was told and climbing aboard his vessel he began the procedures to ready the helicopter for takeoff. Wes was unsure why the pilot followed his command without a question. It occurred to him that if he was in the pilot's shoes and just witnessed two people dying then he also would want to be leaving as fast as possible. Who knew what else was to come?

The helicopter began to take flight as he sat in the back. He was unable to come to terms with what had just happened. Everything since arriving at the prison had seemed like a horrible dream and he almost expected to wake up and find himself home in bed at the little apartment he had shared with Scott. Unfortunately, he did not rouse from a dream. Instead he was met with the views of burning buildings as the aircraft flew over the prison. They were too high and it was too dark to make out the small stuff, all that could be seen below was the glow of fires that dotted the landscape that had been started by the war that was taking place below.

All that was left for Wes to do was to hold it together until he arrived back in civilization. That would not be the end of his journey, though. He still had to find his way home and that would prove to be a difficult task when the only things he had in his possession were the clothes on his back. However, the hard part was finished. He was now the third person to ever escape Uranium City Prison.

His hands were feeling slightly cold. In an attempt to warm them he proceeded to stick them in the shelter of his coat pocket. Doing so, he felt a piece of paper and remembered the envelope Scott had handed him just before he died. He pulled it from his pocket. Enclosed was a picture. The front was facing away from him when he drew out the photo and he saw a small amount of writing on the back which he read before flipping it over to view the image in the photograph.

> *Wes,*
>
> *I made a mistake and I am sorry. If you are reading this then I succeeded in reaching you, however I am probably dead. I was tricked into giving you up to a man calling himself Abhorson. He had told me that he was an old relative of yours and wanted to meet with you in private to discuss some family affairs. So, on the night you were taken I left home and went to the bar for a few drinks. When I returned the place*

> *was trashed. With a lot of digging and after calling in a few favors from some friends who have a few high connections, I was able to discover who Abhorson was and where he may have taken you. I was unable to figure out why he took you to Uranium City but I did discover why you were the one he chose.*
>
> *The picture will explain and I wish you good luck in finding your way home.*
>
> *-Scott*

Turning the photograph over Wes realized why Abhorson looked so familiar to him when they were on the bus as it headed towards the prison. The picture was one from his personal photo album. In the picture were two people - his mother while she was pregnant and her husband, a man he now knew by the name Abhorson.

The End

Made in the USA
Charleston, SC
10 December 2014